REVELING IN SIN

SIN TRILOGY BOOK THREE

MEGHAN

NEW YORK TIMES BESTSELLING AUTHOR

MARCH

CONTENTS

REVELING IN SIN

Book Three of the Sin Trilogy

Meghan March

ALSO BY MEGHAN MARCH

Sin Trilogy:

Richer Than Sin

Guilty As Sin

Reveling In Sin

Mount Trilogy:

Ruthless King

Defiant Queen

Sinful Empire

Savage Trilogy:

Savage Prince

Iron Princess

Rogue Royalty

Beneath Series:

Beneath This Mask

Beneath This Ink

Beneath These Chains

Beneath These Scars

Beneath These Lies

Beneath These Shadows

Beneath The Truth

ABOUT THIS BOOK

Whitney Gable is the kind of woman you fight to the death to protect.

To keep.

To cherish.

I've finally learned my lesson, and it's time to prove I'm the man who's worthy of her.

I don't care what it takes, because failure is not an option.

No matter who or what stands in our way—this time, she'll be mine forever.

Reveling in Sin is the third and final book in the Sin Trilogy.

WHITNEY

Ten years ago

My palms turned clammy as I stood in the back room of the small church. I didn't remember the ride here or even changing from my street clothes into this dress.

Actually, I didn't really remember picking out the dress either. Everything that had happened in the weeks since my parents' accident had been a blur.

When I lifted my gaze to the mirror in front of me, I barely recognized the girl staring back at me. My reflection was pale, with dark circles under my eyes. Even the makeup I'd caked on this morning couldn't hide how I felt. My face looked thin; my stomach had been twisted into so many knots lately that I'd had trouble forcing myself to eat.

I'd asked for a moment of privacy before it was time to walk down the aisle to the man I didn't want to marry, and thankfully Jackie, Cricket, and Karma all left me alone.

Now I stood in silence, dressed in white, wondering how the hell I'd let things get so messed up.

One word formed in my brain and grew louder and louder with each passing second.

Run!

My gaze swung to the small frosted windowpane above the pastor's desk. It was the only way out of the room other than the door leading into the church—where there was no chance I could escape unnoticed. If I ditched the dress, I might fit through the window . . .

My feet moved of their own volition, taking me nearer to the frosted glass and possible freedom.

And then what would I do? Run to Lincoln? Tell him he was going to lose everything he'd been groomed to inherit for his entire life because I couldn't go through with marrying a man I didn't love?

The door opened with a soft click before I could make a decision.

I spun around to see Ricky's mom—the woman completely responsible for me standing here today. She couldn't have maneuvered me more effectively if she'd had a gun to my head.

Her gaze shifted from me to the window and back to me again. The cruel curve of her smile yanked the knots in my stomach even tighter.

"The window? Really? So dramatic. I know what you're thinking, Whitney. All you have to do is run to him and the prince will save you." Her flinty green gaze hardened. "That's not how this works. When he finds out that you could've saved his perfect little life and his inheritance, but you didn't, he's going to think you're a selfish whore. He'll hate you for the rest of his life. Is that what you want?"

"He couldn't possibly hate me as much as I hate you," I whispered.

"I don't like you either, but as long as my son says you're his one-way ticket to rock-stardom, I'll suck it up." She flicked her gaze toward the window again with a shake of her head. "That Riscoff boy doesn't love you. You're just the first cheap and easy lay he found when he got back to town. He was going to throw you away as soon as he got tired of you. And now, he'll move on as soon as you're gone."

Her words sent a razor-sharp swipe across my heart. "You don't know that."

"I know that there's only one thing that matters to the Riscoffs—winning." She stepped closer, crumpling the white skirt of my dress as she invaded my personal space. "If he shows up here today, you'd better make it a good show. Make him believe that you're done with him. Because if you don't, I'll destroy him and his family. Just watch and see."

The gleefully evil smile that settled on Renee's face reinforced the point she'd already driven home—she was crazy enough to do what she threatened. If I hadn't believed that from the beginning, I would have gone to Lincoln.

But now, there was only one option left for me. Obey and pray.

"I'm here, aren't I? I'm doing what you want."

"Good. I'm glad you get it." Renee tilted her head, and her perfectly coifed mother-of-the-groom hair didn't move an inch. She was a pretty woman. Still relatively young-

3

looking for having a twenty-seven-year-old son, but there was something hard and brittle about the set of her mouth and the sharpness of her eyes.

Brittleness that no doubt came from being used up by Roosevelt Riscoff.

"He'll hide you away just like his father hid me until he pays you off to stay quiet about it ever happening."

Renee's bitter words from the morning she confessed her dirty secrets ran through my head, as did Lincoln's from the last night I saw him.

"I want to take care of you, Whitney. Let me."

As much as I wished I could stand here and tell Renee Rango to go to hell, because Lincoln would never treat me the same way his father treated her, I couldn't deny that I'd already walked away from him for making the very same suggestion. He'd find me a house. Pay my bills. Give me spending money. *Leave me bitter and jaded when he got tired of me.*

No matter what I did, it was a risk. The only thing I knew for certain? If I walked out of this church without marrying Ricky, Renee Rango would destroy everything Lincoln had ever cared about.

I couldn't let that happen.

I would stand by the decision I made—I'd save Lincoln's future by marrying Ricky.

That didn't mean I had to like it.

I lifted my chin and met Renee's stare. "Get out of my sight. I don't want to see you again until this is over."

Her lips quirked up and her smile turned even more vicious. "I don't give a damn what you want. You'll do what I say or face the consequences." She moved toward the door. "I'll leave you to get yourself ready for your . . . performance."

As soon as Renee stepped out of the room, Jackie slipped in.

"Are you okay, Whit? You look even paler than you did before."

I wanted to tell Aunt Jackie everything, but I bit my tongue until the sting brought tears to my eyes.

"Can I have a tissue?"

Aunt Jackie frowned and reached for the box on top of the piano next to the pastor's desk. "Of course. What's wrong? Are you having second thoughts?"

Second thoughts? I wanted to say. *More like fifth, sixth, and seventh thoughts.* But I didn't. I just shook my head as I dabbed carefully at my eyes.

"You know you're making the right choice, don't you, sweet girl? I know you thought you had something with that Riscoff boy, but it wasn't going to end with a white dress in a church and vows in front of your entire family."

I lifted my gaze to hers. "Why would you say that? How can you possibly know?"

"Gables and Riscoffs never end well together." She paused, and I wondered if she was thinking about my mom, because she'd been on my mind nonstop today.

What advice would my mother have given me? I would never know . . . because she died with a Riscoff. My stomach flipped again, and this time bile burned as it climbed up my throat. Aunt Jackie didn't seem to notice, though, and she kept speaking.

"Feuds don't last a hundred seventy years without there being plenty of hostility on both sides. It would take a hell of a lot more than some Romeo-and-Juliet kind of love story to end this one. I know you want to be the exception to the rule, Whitney. I understand. I get it. But you can't be that naive. He's too young and reckless to pin your hopes on. You just happened to be the first girl in Gable he picked. That doesn't mean you'd be the last. As a matter of fact, I'd be willing to put money on it."

"But—" I tried to interrupt and tell her she didn't know Lincoln like I did.

"No buts, girl. You're smarter than that. At best, he'll pay all your bills so you're around whenever he needs you to get off. But you're not a whore, Whitney. You're better than that. Why would you let a man buy you when you have a good one waiting outside that door who wants to marry you and treat you like a queen?"

I hated the comparison she threw down, because it played into all the insecurities Lincoln and Renee had dredged up. But still . . . that didn't change the facts.

"I don't love Ricky." I lifted my gaze to Jackie's and expected to find her face stricken, but I was wrong. There wasn't a single trace of shock in her expression.

"You only think that matters because you're still too innocent to know any different. You don't have to love him to use him as your ticket out of this town. He's already got a song on the radio, and we both know why that is. Use your brain, Whitney. You get him more songs on the radio, get that money rolling in, learn to play the game, and you're going to be taken care of forever. This is the best life I could hope for you to have. Don't screw it up over something as stupid as love."

My last hope of avoiding my fate evaporated like drops of rain on desert sand. There wasn't a single person in this church who would understand me if I ran out the front door instead of rushing down the aisle to say my vows to a rising rock star.

But even if I did, it wouldn't change anything. I had to marry Ricky to save Lincoln.

My only choice was clear.

"Now, you about ready to get this done with?"

I'll never be ready, I thought, *but it doesn't matter.*

I met Aunt Jackie's gaze and lied. "I'm ready."

My aunt pressed a kiss to my forehead. "Good girl. Your mama would be proud. I'll go get your brother, and we can get this over with before anything goes wrong."

WHITNEY

WITH EVERY STEP down the aisle of the church, I dreamed of someone rushing in to save me. Not just *someone*. One very specific person. But when Asa kissed my forehead and handed me over to Ricky, my stomach knotted once more.

No one was coming to save me, because I was doing the saving.

Ricky said his vows and the preacher moved on to me. I must have said the right things, because he nodded approvingly.

That's when it happened.

The doors to the church flung open and everyone inside spun around, me included.

Oh, Lord in heaven.

Instead of Lincoln sweeping in to carry me off like a white knight, he stumbled through the doors wearing clothes that looked like he'd slept in them for a week. His jaw was covered with thick stubble, and his eyes were so bloodshot, I could see the redness from twenty-five feet away.

"I object." The words came out slurred, and there was no question he was completely hammered.

For some reason, that fact hit me like a backhand to the face. My white knight, my love, my savior . . . showed up to interrupt my wedding *drunk.*

Because I'm not the kind of girl who gets carried off into the sunset by a prince on a stallion. I'm a Gable.

When Renee Rango stepped toward the aisle, I knew I had to react quickly before she pulled the pin on the truth grenade she was using to hold me hostage.

I whirled around and marched down the aisle toward Lincoln. To fuel the authenticity of my anger, I focused on the fact that *he showed up drunk.*

"You *asshole.* How *dare* you?"

"You can't marry him." Lincoln could barely stand upright, and his words were one step above gibberish.

In that moment, a memory burst into my head—my dad showing up wasted at my spring formal to drag my mom, who was acting as a chaperone, out of the gym because he thought she was flirting with one of my classmates. I grasped onto that memory with everything I had, even though Lincoln was nothing like my dad. I had to use it to make this seem genuine.

I have no other choice. Every second Lincoln stood in this church was one moment closer to Renee Rango destroying his entire life.

"I don't know why you think you get to have an opinion, but get the hell out of here."

Lincoln stumbled forward another step. "I can buy and sell him."

Why did he have to go there? Why does everything always have to be about money?

"I. Don't. Care. Because *you can't buy* me."

Before I could finish my sentence, Asa and Ricky rushed by me and shoved Lincoln out the front doors of the church.

I never got to say my true thoughts.

My love is free.

LINCOLN

Present day

"MOTHER WAS PRONOUNCED dead at the hospital a half hour ago. Heart attack. They couldn't resuscitate her. You fucking killed her. I hope you're happy."

My brother's caustic tone coming through the phone shreds my hope that I misheard him.

This can't be happening. She can't be . . .

"If this is some sick stunt you're trying to pull—"

"You're the one who pulled the stunt, big brother, and this is what you got in return. Good job. Son of the fucking year. Don't bother coming back from wherever you ran off to with your whore. Mom wouldn't want you here anyway." Harrison's rage comes through loud and clear before he ends the call, and I'm left with nothing but silence.

Whitney looks at me, all color drained from her face. "Oh my God. Oh my God. I'm so sorry. I shouldn't have—"

I hold up a hand because I don't want to hear her say what I know she's going to say. That she shouldn't have come with me. That I shouldn't have picked her over my mother. That none of this ever should have happened.

Disbelief and anger charge through my system with equal jolts of power. Part of me thinks this is some elaborate ploy by my mother and brother to lure me back and convince me to abandon Whitney, but the other part . . . the other part can't believe I've just lost my only remaining parent.

I squeeze my eyes shut and take two long deep breaths as shards of guilt, pain, and self-disgust dig deeper into me with each hammering beat of my heart.

I did this. This is my fault. My choice pushed her over the edge.

When I open my eyes, I look out at the ocean and focus on the deep blue of the waves lapping against the sea wall.

But I find no comfort there. Blue House has been robbed of the peace it usually provides.

"I'm so sorry, Lincoln. So damn sorry. I never should have—"

Whitney starts again, but this time I wrap my arms around her and yank her against my body to cut off her words. I hold her tight, rocking us both back and forth as I let the news sink in.

My mother is gone.

My mother's last wish was to keep Whitney and me apart, and she made her final stand in a way that no one could have predicted. We've always thought it was theatrics and manipulation. Her health was the card she played to keep us in line, but there was never a real threat to her life—or so we'd believed.

I never thought . . .

I draw in breath after breath, but this feels completely surreal. Like a joke Harrison is playing because he's pissed at me. But even he wouldn't lie about this.

My mother is gone.

I shake my head as I silently flay myself. *I'm so sorry, Mother. Sorry I couldn't be the son you needed. Sorry you didn't get the life you wanted. Sorry that I couldn't help you find a way to let go of the past and your bitterness.*

I pull back and look down at Whitney. "I can't apologize for loving you. I won't." I blink twice as moisture gathers at the corners of my eyes.

"But—"

"You can use this as a reason to push me away, and I'll understand, but the place I need you right now is at my side. Can you do that for me?"

Whitney's teeth drag across her lower lip and apprehension creases her expression. For a few long moments, I expect her to tell me she can't do this. Can't face what has just happened. But she continues to amaze me.

"Whatever you need, Lincoln, I'm here."

I squeeze her tighter against me, letting my grief batter me. It's more savage and unpredictable than the waves rolling in, and I know it will last for years, if not forever. My father's death changed the course of my life and how I lived it. Only time will tell how my mother's passing will change things.

As much as I wish I could hide away from the world and pretend this didn't happen, that's not possible.

I thread my fingers through Whitney's and curl our hands into a solid fist. "We have to go back."

She nods. "I know."

"Then we go back together."

"Only if that's what you want," she says.

What I really want is for the clock to turn back and to find some way to make my mother understand that my falling in love with Whitney Gable was a cause for celebration, not outrage. But that's impossible, and now the only thing I can do is move forward and face the consequences.

With my head buzzing and the sound of my heartbeat thundering in my ears, I lead Whitney back toward the chopper as I wave at the pilot before he can take off. He shuts down the rotors and removes his headset.

"Sir?"

"We need to go back to Gable. To the hospital. There's been an emergency."

WHITNEY

WHEN THE CHOPPER touches down on the helipad in front of the Riscoff Memorial Hospital, my stomach tumbles until I'm afraid I might be sick. How I'm feeling has nothing to do with the helicopter ride and everything to do with the fact that my actions led us here. If I hadn't come back to Gable to begin with . . . if I'd said no to Lincoln . . .

I have so many regrets, but what he said to me on the island keeps running through my head on repeat.

"I can't apologize for loving you."

No matter how insensitive it sounds, I can't apologize for loving him either. I can't deny pulling away from him was my first instinct, though. But what good would it do? Despite the guilt threatening to drown me, I know Lincoln is feeling everything even more acutely. If he's not pushing me away because of what happened, how could I dare do it to him? I can't.

This is my chance to prove that I can stand at his side

and show the world we're stronger together. Our first test starts now.

Lincoln releases my sweaty palm to climb out of the helicopter first. When he holds out his hand to help me exit, I take it and hold tight.

Barricades have been set up around the emergency room entrance, but they don't stop the sound of the press yelling questions and the cameras from flashing.

I pretend I'm blind and deaf, a trick I picked up years ago, and walk straight forward, one foot after another, never letting go of Lincoln's hand. Apprehension wraps tighter around my chest with each step, but I don't let it show.

I remember how I felt the last time I approached this very door at his side. I was terrified that something horrible had happened, but part of me had refused to believe it was possible. This time, I already know that we're walking into a terrible tragedy.

The man I love just lost his mother because he chose me over her.

She had a heart attack that killed her *because of me.* Or rather, her outrage over me.

I still can't quite grasp how someone could hate me so much, but it doesn't matter what I can or can't grasp. It happened, and now it's time to face the consequences.

As soon as we enter the hospital, the doors whoosh shut behind us and the lobby is empty but for a woman with two kids and a man whose hand is wrapped in a towel. At least, until Harrison steps out of the wide double doors that lead into the treatment rooms of the ER. His features contort with rage.

"You've gotta be fucking kidding me. Her body is still

warm, and you're bringing your whore into the hospital with you?"

Commodore rolls out behind Harrison and smacks him in the chest. "Hold your tongue, boy. This isn't the time or the place." The old man looks at Lincoln. "You need to say your good-byes quickly. They need to . . . move her."

I loosen my grip on Lincoln's hand so he can walk ahead of me, but Lincoln squeezes back tighter. *Stronger together,* I remind myself.

"Thank you for waiting for me, sir."

Commodore inclines his head, and Lincoln walks us past Harrison.

"I can't believe he's going to take her in there. Mother would—"

"Enough," Commodore snaps, and Harrison actually listens. "This family has lost too much. Today is for mourning. Tomorrow, you can have your anger. Then we all need to try to find some peace."

With my hand clasped firmly in Lincoln's, I follow him into the room where his sister sits beside a sheet-covered body. McKinley lifts her tear-streaked face, and another swell of guilt hits me.

Lincoln doesn't release his hold on me until McKinley rises from her seat. She throws herself into her big brother's arms.

"She's *gone.* Just like Father. She was fine . . . and then she was *gone.*"

The anguished words hollow me out until my knees threaten to give way. I step back, intent on making myself as small as possible in the corner of the room. Regret pummels me as I watch them grieve the loss of their only remaining parent.

"I'm so sorry, Mac. So sorry."

"I don't know what happened. She was arguing with me, and she just seemed to lose it . . . Then she collapsed, but it wasn't like the other times. I knew this was really bad."

Lincoln's features pinch with pain, and I hate that I know what he's thinking. *She was arguing with McKinley about us.*

"I'm sorry I wasn't here," he says, holding his sister close as she soaks his shirt with her tears.

Last time I was in this hospital, I was the girl who had just become an orphan. Today, that girl is McKinley, and I wish I could spare her the grief that I've felt for the last decade. The edges may dull, but the pain never goes away. And the guilt. *Lord, the guilt.* I don't know if that ever fades, because mine hasn't.

A noise comes from the hall, and we all look toward the doorway to see a man in a white coat peeking his head into the room. "I'm so sorry to interrupt. I'll come back when you're . . . finished."

McKinley releases Lincoln, swiping at her eyes. "We're almost done. My brother just got here to say his good-byes. We won't be long."

When the man disappears from the room, Lincoln's attention shifts to the sheet.

McKinley sniffles. "We want to donate her tissue and whatever else might be able to help someone, if possible, so they need to take her as soon as possible. We waited as long as we could for you."

Lincoln grimaces, and again, I know what he's think ing. He would have been closer by if not for needing to run away with me.

At least he didn't miss his only chance to say good-bye to his mother. I never could have forgiven myself for that. Actually, the chance that I'll be able to forgive myself for any of this is slim to none. No matter what Lincoln says, this will always be my fault. Loving him doesn't change the fact that I'm cursed.

Lincoln reaches for the sheet and stops. He glances over his shoulder at McKinley and me. "Could you both give me a minute? I . . . I'd like to be alone for a moment."

"Of course," his sister says.

I nod because I can't get any words out of my constricted throat.

When I walk toward the door, Lincoln reaches out to snag my hand, pulling me to a stop. "I'll be right out. I'm sorry . . . I just need to . . ."

I swallow past the lump in my throat. "It's fine. Take all the time you need. I'll be here."

LINCOLN

I LOWER MYSELF into the seat McKinley vacated, and my shoulders roll forward. Tears I've been holding back sneak out of my eyes and drip down my cheeks, landing one by one on the white sheet.

"I'm sorry, Mother. It doesn't matter how many times I say it, I'll never be able to tell you that again."

I lift my hand to raise the sheet, but my fingers shake. Once I see her face, it will all become real, and that's not something I want to believe right now. But I don't have a choice.

When I pull back the sheet, I'm prepared for how different she looks, because I remember my dad. The tubes and leads they used to try to save her are still there.

Part of me hoped her face would be placid and peaceful, but it's lined with pain.

I cover her again almost as quickly and bow my head.

"I'm sorry I couldn't be the son you wanted. I'm sorry you felt cheated by life. I'm sorry I could never make you proud of me. I'm sorry I couldn't make you happy. I'm just so fucking sorry, Mother."

The door opens, but I don't look behind me as the power chair rolls inside. I expected him to come.

"You didn't do this to her, so don't you dare blame yourself." Commodore's commanding tone can't make his words the truth, however.

I turn and look at him. My grandfather seems to have aged five years in mere days.

"She made me choose, and I didn't choose her. How could I not blame myself?"

My grandfather shifts in his seat. "She didn't have the right to make you choose. That was her last attempt at manipulating you. Besides," he says as he pulls a newspaper from his seat and holds it out to me. "This is what sent her over the edge. Not you."

I take the paper and read the headline.

BILLIONAIRE'S DEAD SON OUTED AS BIGAMIST

"HOLY FUCK," I whisper.

"Exactly. I need you to say your good-byes to your mother and forgive her for all the heartache she caused you in life and in death. Then you're going to stand up and help me save what's left of this family before Renee Rango destroys us all."

WHITNEY

"You did this," Harrison says to me as Commodore disappears inside the room with Lincoln. "You killed her just as much as he did."

My gaze darts toward him, and McKinley stiffens next to me.

Lincoln's brother doesn't need to lay on the guilt. I'm already feeling plenty. But that doesn't mean I'm going to let him bully me.

I cross my arms over my chest. "What are you talking about?"

He whips out a newspaper from beneath his arm and shoves it at me. As soon as I read the headline, my knees buckle.

"Oh my God," I whisper as the edges crumple in my fingers.

I sacrificed ten years of my life to keep this secret . . . and it was all for nothing.

My second thought hits just as hard. *Roosevelt's shoddy lawyer must not have filed their divorce papers . . . or was Renee lying about him divorcing her too?*

"You knew, didn't you?" Harrison's voice carries a vicious edge.

"Stop it. Just leave her alone." McKinley comes to my rescue and takes the paper from my hand, then tosses it back at her brother. "Ignore him. He's looking for anyone to blame but the person actually responsible for all of it."

I curl my hands into fists and lean against the wall, wanting to scream and rage. But I don't, because I know Harrison will use anything I say against me. Instead, I practice breathing slowly, in through my nose and out through my mouth, to prevent myself from losing my shit.

A few minutes later, the door to the room opens and Lincoln and his grandfather emerge. Lincoln moves to my side and slips his arm around my shoulders.

"It's time to circle the wagons," Commodore announces. "Everyone is going back to the estate, and that's where we'll stay until we've dealt with this situation. If anyone has a problem with that—I don't give a damn."

Lincoln's hold tightens on me as my stomach drops.

Stay at the Riscoff estate with Lincoln's family? Based on the glare Harrison is shooting in my direction, that prospect sounds like a disaster waiting to happen.

"I have to be at the resort," McKinley says. "There's no way I can—"

"Did you not hear me, girl? This isn't up for debate."

McKinley's mouth snaps shut as Commodore barks at her.

Every possible objection I could voice trembles on my tongue, but I hold them back. Better to acquiesce now so I can have this discussion alone with Lincoln later. He'll understand that I can't stay, because I need to track down Ricky's mom and find out why the hell she's doing this.

When no further protests are made, Commodore gives us a final nod. "Good. Everyone, back to the estate. Say nothing to anyone, especially the media."

Harrison is the first one to stalk away, and when he pushes through the doors to enter the waiting area, I catch a glimpse of Aunt Jackie. I was texting her as we landed back in Gable, but I didn't expect her to show up here.

Lincoln must feel my body tense, because his fingers curl tighter around me. "What's wrong?"

I incline my head toward the direction his brother just exited. "I need to talk to Jackie. She's out in the waiting room."

"I'll come with you."

My lips press together, and I debate whether that's a good idea. Jackie will undoubtedly have opinions to share that Lincoln may not want to hear.

When I don't move or reply, he releases his hold on me for a moment, but only to stand directly in front of me and grip my shoulders with both hands.

"You're not getting rid of me, Blue. We're in this together. No matter what happens, it's you and me against the world. I'm not going to lose you now. Whatever comes next, we deal with it together. Nothing breaks us."

His words should give me comfort, but instead, they drive home exactly how much I have to lose. Lincoln doesn't know the secret I've been keeping for ten years. The one that could change everything between us. *And I can't tell him right now.* It isn't the time or the place.

Instead, I settle for nodding and taking as much comfort as I can from the way he threads his fingers through mine as we walk into the waiting room. Lincoln doesn't release my hand until Aunt Jackie rushes forward to hug me.

"I'm sorry I didn't get your calls sooner. We were in the air—"

Jackie cuts me off. "Renee Rango is in town. I just heard."

"Where? We need to find her," Lincoln says as I step back.

Jackie directs her answer to me. "I don't know yet, but I have to believe she's going to be looking for Whitney." Her tone matches her grim expression.

"She's not getting anywhere near Whitney. She'll have to go through me first." Lincoln pulls me into his side.

I meet Aunt Jackie's gaze and find knowledge there I didn't expect. *Does she know that Renee threatened me and that's why I married Ricky? Has she known this whole time?*

Commodore's power chair stops beside us, and I can't ask any of the questions swirling in my brain. "Ms. Gable, you're supposed to be at the resort, where you'll continue to be a guest for as long as this media circus continues."

"Are you telling me I can't leave The Gables?" Jackie asks, her shoulders going back. I recognize her battle posture.

"I'm telling you to be smart with your actions—and your words."

Jackie's gaze narrows on him. "And if I want to go home and get back to my normal life instead of hide from this mess?"

"That's not possible. Security is assigned to your

house, and they're under orders to keep everyone out, including you."

Oh shit is all I can think when Commodore speaks. This isn't going to end well.

"Listen to me, old man." Jackie takes two steps toward him. "If I want to go home, I will."

Commodore folds his hands in his lap, and instead of yelling, his tone is calmer than ever. "If you want your house to still be standing when this is all over, you won't defy me. Now, go back to work."

Jackie's mouth drops open, and I'm sure my face looks the same. "What are you going to do? Burn it down like you did the family farm?"

Commodore's expression betrays nothing, but his words reveal all. "I didn't need to burn down the farm when your brother did it himself out of spite."

"I don't believe you," Jackie snaps as Lincoln's grand-father's accusation burns in my brain.

My dad burned down the farm? And then blamed the Riscoffs?

I don't know why I'm surprised, but I am. All these years, I've thought one thing, and it turns out that the truth is the opposite of what I thought.

"I don't give a damn what you believe, Ms. Gable," Commodore says as he rolls around Jackie. "It doesn't change the truth. Don't be stupid. You have a great job and an extended invitation to live in luxury. Accept it and don't argue."

Jackie's jaw tightens, and I know she wants to go ballistic on Commodore, but somehow she keeps herself together. To Commodore's back, she says, "I don't take orders from you, Mr. Riscoff. I never have and never will.

Whatever I choose to do will be my decision." Her gaze flicks to me. "Whit, we need to talk. *Now.*"

Commodore spins around in his chair with a quiet buzz. "Your niece is under the protection of my family. If you have information that impacts the situation, I need to know." His dark gaze moves between Jackie and me, as though he's ready to start an interrogation.

"Enough," Lincoln says. "We'll have this conversation privately. Not here. Not now. Let's go."

"This can't wait," Jackie says.

Commodore crosses his arms over his chest. "Then tell us all."

Jackie looks around the room, and Lincoln's right. We have a small audience, and whatever Jackie is going to say, now isn't the time. However, that doesn't stop her from delivering a message I don't want to hear.

"Renee Rango's in town. I've been told she's here to serve Whitney with a lawsuit."

"What?" I gasp.

Lincoln pulls me even tighter to his side. "What kind of lawsuit?"

"Wrongful death. She's saying Whitney's at fault for Ricky's suicide."

LINCOLN

WHITNEY SITS SILENTLY beside me as we ride back to the estate. She hasn't said anything since we left the hospital.

"If there's really a lawsuit, we'll fight it, and we'll win. There's nothing to worry about," I tell her as we approach the bridge.

"You don't know that. Renee . . . she's . . ." Whitney takes a deep breath.

"She's what?" I ask.

I wait while Whitney gathers her thoughts and turns in her seat. Her troubled blue gaze meets mine.

"She's crazy. Like completely off-her-rocker, batshit crazy. You don't understand how nuts she is. There's literally nothing I wouldn't put past her. She swore she would never let any of this go public if I did what she wanted . . ."

The blood pumping through my veins seems to slow as my brain locks onto the last part of what Whitncy said. From the worry stamped on her features, I know it's important.

"What did she want you to do?"

Whitney closes her eyes and swallows, and I brace myself for what's coming next.

"She wanted me to make Ricky a rock star. Write his songs. Make sure his career took off like it did with his first song. She said if I didn't do what she wanted, she would tell everyone about who his father really was, and . . ."

Realization hits me with the force of a dam breach as she trails off, gathering the courage to finish. But I don't need her to finish. My brain is already jumping to conclusions.

For ten years, I haven't been able to figure out what would make Whitney not only go back to Ricky after he cheated, but *actually marry him*. Now I have the piece of the puzzle I've been missing for a decade.

Renee Rango and her threats. That bitch. She stole ten years of the life I wanted, and I'm not going to let her take another second.

"She wanted you to marry him and make him a star . . . and if you didn't, she was going to expose her marriage to my father and tell everyone Ricky was his legitimate son and heir?"

Whitney nods, tears turning her eyes glassy. "She said she'd destroy your family, and that Ricky would get everything and you'd get nothing. I knew if he inherited, he'd run the company into the ground, and every single person who relied on your family for a paycheck would've been ruined too. I couldn't let that happen."

The magnitude of what she did, *for me*, is astounding.

"You married him to save my family. To save me." I say it out loud because I need to hear it to make it real.

Whitney nods. "Yes."

The impact of a single word has never been stronger.

"Jesus Christ." I bring a hand to my face and cover my mouth.

Whitney's gaze drops to her lap. "You have to understand, between your mom and Renee, there was no chance anyone would let us be together, so I did what I thought was right. I hoped if I could just keep Renee and Ricky happy, they'd leave you alone . . . but it wasn't enough. Renee won't stop. Now all she cares about is money, and she'll destroy everything in her path to get it."

I wrap both arms around Whitney and lift her into my lap. "Why didn't you tell me? We could have figured it out together. Commodore would've crushed her before he'd let her take down Riscoff Holdings. And he sure as hell never would've let Ricky inherit a damn thing if he didn't think he would be a decent CEO. He wasn't even going to let my dad have the company."

Whitney's shocked gaze collides with mine. "What? I thought . . . I thought the tradition was impossible to change."

"Turns out Commodore doesn't give a shit about tradition when it's weighed against keeping the company out of the wrong hands. I can't believe you did that for me, for us. Jesus Christ, Blue. Why?"

She lays her head on my shoulder. "Because I loved you too much to let her ruin your life, and I had the chance to stop her. So I did."

Ten years ago, I thought Whitney deserted me for another man, but she did something so much bigger. She gave up *us* to save *me*.

"I didn't deserve you then, just like I don't deserve you now. I'm so sorry you thought you had to do it."

"Don't say that. I don't want it to all have been for nothing. I kept her away for ten years, but I just couldn't handle it anymore. Not after Ricky . . ." Whitney pauses, and I can't let her go on.

"No matter what happens next, I will protect you. And someday, I'm going to prove I'm worthy of you."

We ride in silence the rest of the way to the estate. As we approach the gate, the SUV slows to navigate the throng of reporters who are all crowded around something —not the gate, but a car parked on the side of the road with a redhead standing next to it.

"What the hell is going on?"

Whitney lifts her head and follows my gaze out the window. "*Shit.* Jackie was right. Renee is back, and she's here."

WHITNEY

EVEN THOUGH I haven't seen her brassy red head in months, I would recognize Renee Rango anywhere. There's no mistaking her in the middle of the swarm of reporters outside the gates of the Riscoff estate, although I wish I was wrong.

Nerves buzz to life like little soldiers ready to hold the line, because every time I face Renee, it's a battle. And this time, I have no doubt she's out for blood. My last encounter with her started and ended with her accusing me of murdering her son, in front of two police officers and the coroner, while I was making a positive ID of Ricky's body.

I'll never forget the way her shrieks of *"Arrest her now!"* echoed off the walls of the morgue as security escorted her out of the building. Even now, my hackles rise at the memory of her voice.

When Ricky's lawyer called to tell me that I wasn't invited to the reading of his will, I wasn't surprised. I knew Renee would do everything she could to make my life hell after he was gone. But I learned too late how effectively she'd plotted her revenge. She made sure Ricky not only named her as executor of his estate, but also the sole beneficiary.

When I asked how that was possible, because California is a community property state, the lawyer spouted a bunch of legal jargon at me that I didn't understand. The bottom line, though? He said community property wasn't even a concern at this point because Ricky had spent every penny, and if I wanted to contest the will, all I'd be arguing over was inheriting half the debts Ricky left behind.

The one exception? The house had been purchased in my name, so Renee couldn't throw me out. I stayed in LA for three months to see if the lawyer was lying, but when they carted off the furniture for auction and the sheriff put the notice on the door, I finally believed he was telling the truth. I was lucky that the house sold to a creepy fan for just enough to cover the balance of the mortgage, so at least I didn't have that debt weighing me down.

Before I left LA, there was one final nail pounded into the coffin of my former life. I called Ricky's manager, and he told me Renee had assigned all future royalties of the songs I'd written to the creditors to keep them from taking *her* house.

It added insult to injury. My hard work for a decade had been used to save *her* lifestyle.

That was also the day Cricket made one last attempt to beg me to come home for her wedding. With nothing to keep me in LA and nowhere else to go, I came running back to Gable.

All these memories coalesce into a ball of fire in my

chest, and I want to do nothing more than rip Renee Rango's fake red hair out by the roots.

My visions of petty revenge fade away when Lincoln sits straighter beside me.

"I remember her," he says as he stares out the window. "From years ago. She showed up at the house once to see my father, and my mother ordered her off the property. Fuck, I never put it together."

The gates open as the SUV ahead of us, carrying Commodore and McKinley, slips inside and we follow, leaving the muted voices of various members of the press behind us. The thought of what Renee Rango is telling them sends my apprehension even higher.

No matter what Lincoln said about protecting me from Renee, I know how ruthless she can be.

When we climb out of the SUV, Lincoln waits for his grandfather to be assisted into his power chair before he speaks.

"We need to exhume my father's body and perform the DNA test. I don't trust Renee Rango, and if there's a shred of a chance that she might be lying about all of this, we need to know now so we can shut her down."

Commodore settles into his chair and maneuvers it to face us. "I agree. We'll do it tomorrow morning. It's time to lay this to rest, once and for all."

LINCOLN

RENEE RANGO HAS SHOT straight to the top of my list of people I despise. I will never forget that she took ten years from Whitney and me, and I wasn't even aware she did it. To me, that makes her a very real and dangerous adversary.

Ricky Rango's mother is about to become well acquainted with an indisputable fact of my life—no one fucks with what matters to me and gets away with it, and Whitney matters more than anything.

Commodore withdraws to his old office when we enter the house, and Whitney and I follow my sister into the drawing room where she powers on her laptop. I don't know where the hell my brother is, and right now, I don't care.

"Find out if they're filming Renee Rango out front," I say to McKinley. "Check the gossip sites. Someone has to be live streaming."

My sister glances back at me. "I was planning on

working. Why don't you use that fancy little box in your hand to do it."

"You're faster on a computer. Besides, damage control comes first. Work can wait."

With a huff, she lets her fingers fly across the keyboard and pulls up three different gossip sites within seconds. Headlines about Ricky Rango are on the front page of all of them, but only one has a live stream.

I point at the rectangle on the screen. "Click there. I want to know what this woman is saying."

McKinley moves the cursor with her finger and clicks. The window fills the screen, and Renee Rango's voice comes from the speakers as she holds her informal press conference outside the gates of our goddamned house.

"Why did I keep silent for so long? I was afraid for my life and for my son's life. There's nothing a mother wouldn't do to protect her child, and you have to take precautions when you're dealing with a family like the Riscoffs who don't think the rules apply to them."

The reporters lap up her bullshit. At least, all but one of them.

"Did the Riscoffs give you money in exchange for your silence? Is that why you really stayed quiet? Because I find it hard to believe you were still afraid for your life and Ricky's after he became a superstar," one man asks pointedly.

The cameras trained on Renee's face show her lips pinching and jaw flexing as he makes his statement.

"Considering you're not female, and you're clearly not a mother, you can't possibly understand the lengths a mother would go to protect her child, no matter how old he is. I wasn't taking any chances. The Riscoffs are—"

A woman cuts her off. "But did they pay you off, Renee?"

Renee's face screws up into a vicious frown. "It was blood money. I took it because I had no choice. Don't you dare judge me."

"And what do you think about the rumors that Whitney Rango, your late son's widow, is now in a relationship with Lincoln Riscoff?"

Renee's gaze sharpens. "I have only one thing to say about that opportunistic, gold-digging whore—*she killed my son*! She may as well have put that needle in his vein. She never should've cheated on him. She did this; she took him from me. And now I'm going to take everything from that lying little c—"

The recording cuts off, and McKinley and I both spin around when we hear a gasp.

Whitney stands behind me, her arms wrapped around her middle. "That *bitch*. That conniving, lying bitch. I never cheated on him!"

I reach out to pull her against me, but Whitney shakes her head.

"I don't need placating. It's time to set the record straight. I'm done letting Renee paint me as the monster here, and the press believing every single word of it. I'm *done*. It's my turn now."

I thread my fingers through hers. "You can have your say, Blue. No question. But how do you want to do it? A press conference? We can set one up for tomorrow."

Whitney shakes her head. "No, I'm doing this right now." She lifts her gaze toward the front of the house. "The press is here. She's here. I'm not letting Renee Rango terrorize me for another goddamned day."

"Are you sure?" I ask.

"This sounds like a really risky idea, Whitney," McKinley says. "Not that I think you shouldn't have your say, but—"

Whitney tugs her fingers from my grip. "It's time. I'm going."

WHITNEY

THE LAST TIME I left the Riscoff estate, I was the disgraced maid who'd been caught screwing around with the heir. This time, I'm walking out the door with Lincoln beside me, his sister behind us, and Commodore watching from the massive front porch. He rolled out of his study just in time to catch my march to the front door, making me wonder if the old man has cameras rigged in the house. Either way, I wasn't going to let him stop me.

I fully expected Commodore would tell me to let the lawyers handle it, and I wasn't allowed to make a statement to the press, but he surprised me by saying, "It's about time you gave them hell, Ms. Gable."

The clasp of Lincoln's hand is strong and warm as I stride toward the gate. Even though fear of the possible repercussions of my actions races through my veins, I'm not going to let it stop me.

What's the worst that can happen? I know I should be careful asking that question, but Lincoln knows why I married Ricky and why I stayed with him. I have no more

39

secrets. Renee and the press can ask anything, and I have nothing to hide.

I do, however, have a hell of a lot to say.

We reach the gate, and it takes only a moment before someone spots the three of us. The members of the media swing around and abandon their focus on Renee, who now stands on top of the hood of a black Kia.

"Whitney! Will you answer questions?"

Lincoln enters a code on the pedestrian gate and it unlocks. He and I step through, but McKinley stays back. The reporters surge forward, trying to get closer to me, but Lincoln holds out a hand.

"Please keep a respectful distance if you want Ms. Gable to answer your questions. The sheriff is on his way, and anyone who gets too close will be spending the night in jail. Do you understand me?"

His authoritative tone booms out, and the reporters nod their heads and take a step back.

Lincoln squeezes my hand. "Ms. Gable has a statement to make, and after that, she may or may not answer questions, so I suggest you remain quiet so you can hear what she has to say."

The crowd in front of the gate falls silent, including Renee Rango, which shocks me. Either she's waiting for a more opportune moment to strike, or she's subdued by Lincoln's threatening tone. Regardless, all eyes are now on me.

I straighten my shoulders and lift my chin.

"For months, I've kept my silence about the events surrounding the death of my husband. I've let you crucify me in your articles and haven't spoken out against a single one of your false accusations. I made that choice, and I've lived with the consequences long enough. Now, I'm breaking that silence to tell you what really happened." They start to murmur to each other, and I add, "If you want the real story behind my marriage to Ricky Rango and how it ended, you're about to get it."

"She's a liar! Don't believe a word she says!" Renee's screech comes out as though on cue.

I point toward where she stands, with her face turning as red as her hair. "That's my former mother-in-law, Renee Rango. When I was twenty-one years old, she coerced me into marrying her son using the threat that if I didn't, she would destroy the Riscoff family."

"Why would she have to force you to marry an up-and-coming rock star?"

I smile sweetly. "Because I dumped him after he cheated on me, but then he realized he wasn't going to have a career without me." I take a deep breath. "You've been lied to for the last decade. Ricky Rango never wrote a single one of his own songs. *I wrote them.*"

The entire crowd goes silent as I drop what might be the biggest news to hit the music industry in years, especially because Ricky was so vocal about his songwriting process and what it meant to be a true artist.

I just turned a legend into a liar with a single truth.

The questions come rapid fire after that.

"You wrote his songs?"

"Why would Ricky lie?"

"Why make the claim now when Ricky can't defend himself?"

"Do you have proof?"

And from Renee, "She's a lying whore! Don't believe a word she says!"

"If you want proof, I have over a decade's worth, including every single draft of every song and all the brainstorming that went into it. No matter what Renee Rango says or what you think, Ricky Rango wasn't the man he showed to the world. When I asked for a divorce, because I found out he'd been cheating, he threatened to kill me. That was your rock legend. He lived a lie, and he died with people believing that lie."

"Why come forward now?"

"Because I'm tired of being the victim. I've spent too long letting other people dictate my life, and I'm taking my power back. Thank you for your time. I'm done here."

I turn, and Lincoln follows at my back as we walk toward the pedestrian gate. McKinley pulls it open from the inside.

The press continues to yell questions until a gunshot explodes.

"Get down!" Lincoln wraps his arms around me and throws us both through the gate. We hit the ground hard and the metal slams shut behind us.

LINCOLN

I USE my body to cover Whitney on the ground and reach out a hand to pull my sister closer. We wait for another shot to come, but all we hear is mass hysteria.

"Get her gun!"

"Don't let her—"

"No!"

That's when the second gunshot comes, and this one is even louder. I brace for impact, but when nothing hits me, I roll off Whitney and maneuver her and McKinley behind the stone column for better cover.

"Stay here. Don't move."

I stand as Commodore zips down the driveway in his power chair, holding his shotgun in his lap.

"No one move," Commodore roars. "The sheriff will be here momentarily to arrest the person who just attempted to murder my grandson."

"Oh my God. Did she hit you?" Whitney whips around, panic in her tone as she scours me for injury.

"No. I'm fine."

MEGHAN MARCH

"My son died because of that little whore," Renee Rango screams. "She doesn't get to live!"

Whitney attempts to peek around the column to see the woman, but I lock my arms around her.

"Don't move until someone has her secured. Don't make yourself an easy target."

"But—" Whitney tries to protest, but I'm not going to take a chance with her. I meet her frantic blue gaze.

"Your life is more important than whatever shit that crazy woman has to spew. I won't let Renee Rango take you from me again. No way in hell."

The crack of another gunshot has me locking my arms tighter around her.

"That bitch!" Commodore yells from the driveway. "She fucking shot me!"

My gaze snaps to my grandfather. His left arm hangs at his side, blood soaking his white shirt.

I kiss Whitney's forehead. "Stay here. Don't move. Got me?"

She nods, and my attention lands on McKinley. Her expression is one I recognize—hard and determined. It's her *shit got real and it's time to lock it down* expression. She reaches out a hand, as if ready to grab Whitney if she tries to run.

I bolt toward my grandfather as he lifts the shotgun with only his right arm. The barrel shakes without a second hand to steady it, but that doesn't stop him from training the gun on Renee.

"Put your goddamn gun down, woman."

The reporters who were standing around her have fled for cover, hiding behind cars and trees.

Wailing sirens grow louder as the sheriff draws closer.

Renee stands in the grass, her gun trained on Commodore —and now me.

"This is all your fault. The great Commodore Riscoff. You're a joke of a man. You're the reason your son abandoned me!"

"Put the gun down, woman, or I'll pull this trigger. No one shoots at my family."

"Give me the gun," I say from behind him. "You're losing too much blood."

"Not a chance in hell. I don't trust that woman not to fire again, and if she does, she's not walking away."

Renee cackles like a crazy woman, which arguably, she is. "Your precious *family*. If you really cared about your family, then you wouldn't have forced your son to marry that woman."

The sheriff's SUV skids to a halt in the middle of the road, but Renee doesn't stop her rant.

"He should've still been *mine*! I'll kill you all for that!"

I reach for the controls on my grandfather's chair and move it to the side as fast as I can before she fires again.

Renee pulls the trigger and another shot immediately follows it, and it didn't come from Commodore's shotgun.

I look up to see Renee Rango on the ground, her gun at her side. The sheriff rushes over to her, speaking into his radio at the same time.

Jesus fuck. What a goddamned mess.

Commodore steers his power chair toward the gate, his bleeding arm pressed to his side. "Everyone in the house. Now."

Despite Commodore's orders, I refuse to leave his side as my sister hustles Whitney up the driveway. Paramedics are on their way, and the gray pallor of my grandfather's skin scares the hell out of me. I'm not about to lose him today too.

"I told you to go in the house," the old man tells me.

"And I've stopped following orders I don't agree with. Feel free to fire me if you have a problem with that."

His bushy white eyebrows draw together as I yank off my shirt, then tear it into strips to wrap them around his arm to stop the bleeding.

"Stubborn SOB," he mutters, and the tone of his voice betrays the pain he's in.

"Just like my grandfather, so I'll take that as a compliment."

A glint of something that looks a hell of a lot like approval shines in his gaze when he looks up at me.

More sirens pierce the air as the deputies arrive, blue and red lights flashing. The reporters have abandoned their cover in favor of snapping as many pictures of the after-math of what happened.

The deputies set up a perimeter and shoo the press away, but they don't stop. They're vultures, just like Whitney said.

Renee Rango might have been crazy, but even she deserves better than that. I stand up to open the gate for the sheriff and yell as it shuts behind him.

"Put your fucking cameras down and have some goddamned respect."

Every head turns in my direction, and I couldn't care less. I return to my grandfather's side while we await the EMTs.

He answers the sheriff's questions about what happened, and I can't help but feel sorry for Renee Rango. Something in her broke a long time ago, and she never recovered.

Or my father broke her.

Just the thought of how many lives his actions have affected makes me vow that I'll never be like him. And now we may never know the whole truth of what happened.

WHITNEY

HARRISON LOOKS up over the edge of his newspaper when McKinley and I return to the drawing room. I didn't want to come in the house. I wanted to stay out front with Lincoln, but McKinley convinced me to come inside by telling me I would just distract him.

"Were those gunshots?" Harrison asks.

"Are you serious? How could you not come out and check on us if you thought you heard gunshots?" McKinley snaps. "Do you really not give a damn about anything but yourself?"

Harrison lowers the paper. "Why would I run *toward* gunshots? I'm not an idiot. Either way, I figured that if Lincoln got shot, someone had to survive to take over the company."

His nonchalant tone and absolute lack of concern makes me want to murder him where he sits. How can he be so callous about the health and safety of his own siblings? I hate thinking of Asa out in the field where he's no doubt dodging bullets regularly. It guts me to think of him in danger.

McKinley lashes out at her brother. "That's all you care about, isn't it? The money you'd inherit if Lincoln died? You disgust me."

"For being smart? I refuse to apologize for that, and it's certainly not disgusting. Father would have approved." He drops his attention back to his paper, and I want to rip it out of his hands and beat him over the head with it.

Harrison reminds me of Karma, and as far as I'm concerned, you don't need enemies when you have family like that.

McKinley swipes her laptop off the table and holds it against her chest. "I hope you can pull your head out of your ass and realize what a dick you're being without us losing another family member. Commodore just got shot, and you haven't even bothered to ask if everyone was okay."

Harrison pops out of his chair. "What the fuck? Is he dead?"

McKinley swings around to face him. "You'd like that, wouldn't you? And no, he's not dead. You think we'd be standing here if he was? What the hell is wrong with you, Harrison?"

Her brother bolts toward the door, and we both watch him go.

"I'll never understand him," McKinley whispers, and that makes two of us.

"Are you sure we shouldn't go back out? Your grandfather—"

"Is as tough as nails," she finishes for me. "Commodore will outlive us all. I'm nearly certain of that."

"But what if they need to take him to the hospital?"

McKinley laughs quietly. "He'll never go. Not for himself. He'll have a doctor here within the next twenty minutes to do whatever needs doing, guaranteed."

I know she's right, and the last thing I want to do is get in the way of the chaos outside—or offer the press more chances to take pictures. But still, it doesn't feel right hiding inside.

"Are you sure?"

McKinley nods. "Absolutely." She strides toward the massive entrance to the room and pauses before it. "You can come with me to the library if you'd like to distract yourself while we wait."

Go with McKinley, or stay and pace the living room by myself and feel completely useless? It's not much of a choice to make.

I follow her out of the room. "Please don't take this the wrong way, but has Harrison always been that big of an asshole? I have a cousin who's angry at the world, and I swear she's been like that since birth."

McKinley walks and talks at the same time. "He used to be different, actually. When we were little, he was fun and nice. I think it all changed when he saw Commodore take extra interest in Lincoln and not him, and when he asked why, my mother told him he wouldn't get anything because Lincoln would inherit everything. I wish she never had. I wish none of us had ever known, because it changed a lot of things."

"But you're not like him . . ."

McKinley shrugs. "I guess I never saw a reason to be bitter. I didn't expect a handout. I expected to work for everything I would ever get, because that's the way

Commodore has always been. Nothing is a given. Everything is earned. I started working at the resort when I was eight. I helped organize name cards and place settings for wedding receptions because I loved to watch the people come in, all dressed up, and then the bride and groom were so happy and in love." She trails off, and it's not a difficult conclusion to come to that she didn't see a lot of love in this house.

"I started working about that age too. On the family farm. I was in charge of collecting eggs and feeding the chickens."

McKinley stops in front of a wooden door that must be at least twenty feet tall. "Were your parents ever happy?"

Part of me is shocked she asked the question, when we both know what happened with my mom and her father. Still, if she can find the guts to ask the question, then I can give her an honest answer.

"No. Not that I remember."

She hugs her laptop to her chest. "I'm never getting married. I'm going to stay firmly in love with my hotel, and that's it."

Her declaration makes me sad, but I can't blame her.

"You might change your mind if the right guy shows you that it can be different."

McKinley pushes open the door, and I'm too dumbstruck by what's beyond it to continue making whatever point I was attempting.

"Holy shit. This is . . . unreal."

McKinley smiles. "It's my favorite place in the house. I used to pretend that I was Belle and trapped in the Beast's castle when I was a kid." She shakes her head. "Let's not dive too deeply into that fantasy, because I'm sure my shrink would have a field day if I ever mentioned it."

"I don't blame you one bit," I tell her in a hushed tone as we walk inside. The room is two stories high, and books line hundreds of shelves. "This is amazing."

She sets up her laptop on a table in front of a window that looks out over the gorge. "I've missed it. I've been working so much at the resort that I barely make it home. Mother was always hounding me to spend more time here, but she made it hard to want to . . ."

McKinley blinks back tears, and for a moment, she looks so much like the young girl that I once protected from bullies that it breaks my heart. It's been hours since she lost her mother, her grandfather just took a bullet, and she's been so strong. It only makes sense that she would break.

"I know you don't know me that well, but can I hug you?" When McKinley nods, I cross the room to wrap my arms around her. "I'm so sorry about your mother. I'm so sorry that—"

"No, please don't apologize," McKinley says on a sniffle. "She shouldn't have put Lincoln in that position. It wasn't fair to him or you or any of us. And then there's whatever my father did or didn't do. So much of this mess rests on his shoulders, and he'll never be able to tell us what really happened."

"I'm still sorry," I whisper and hug her tighter.

She lets a few more tears fall before she pulls back. "Mother wouldn't want me to make a scene out of grief. She'd be disappointed."

"You're entitled to whatever you feel. If you want to scream and take books off the shelves and throw them across the room and break furniture, I'm not going to judge. Feel what you need to feel. Say what you need to say."

McKinley smiles, and her hazel eyes that look so much like Lincoln's shimmer with unshed tears. "You're a good influence, Whitney. I'm glad my brother has you. I'm glad he's brought you into all our lives again." She gives me one last squeeze and lets me go, then settles in front of her computer and gets back to work.

I suppose everyone deals with grief differently, and like I learned last time, life always goes on, no matter what. Even when we don't think it should.

My heart breaks for both our families and all the pain and loss we've had to bear. I think we're all due for a spell of good luck.

If only wishing could make it happen.

LINCOLN

NOT SURPRISINGLY, Commodore refuses to go to the hospital. The bullet grazed his arm, and the wound doesn't look as bad as I expected. Still, I know there's no chance he'll change his mind. I call his doctor, fill him in on the situation, and he promises he'll be at the house within the half hour.

In the middle of my call, my brother finally appears, and of course, nothing he has to say is helpful.

"This is all Whitney Gable's fault! She has to go! This never would have happened if she weren't here. None of this would've—"

"Shut the fuck up, Harrison," I snap as soon as I end the call, and my grandfather turns to look at him as he rolls toward the house.

"I don't want to hear another word out of you for the rest of the goddamned day," Commodore says to my brother as he continues ahead of us, manipulating his chair with his good arm.

As soon as our grandfather is out of earshot, Harrison

starts up again. "I can't believe you brought her here. Mother is screaming from the heavens knowing that woman is in our house. A fucking Gable. Leave it to you to be just like Father. If you think you're going to move her in here like she's lady of the manor—"

My jaw clenches so hard, it threatens to crack my teeth. I speak in a measured tone to make sure my brother doesn't misunderstand me.

"She's here because I want her here, and Commodore wants her here. If you have another thing to say about her, I'll beat the hell out of you in front of all the reporters that are still out front."

Harrison is spoiling for a fight, and I'd be glad to give it to him, but I care a hell of a lot more about making sure Commodore is patched up quickly than I do about sparring with my brother. I leave him behind in the driveway and head inside the house.

After I make sure Martin has made Commodore comfortable while he waits for the doctor, I find McKinley and Whitney in the library after borrowing a fresh shirt. My heart squeezes tighter in my chest when I see how she's watching over my little sister. Thankfully, someone delivered food because it's been a long goddamned day.

I meet Whitney's gaze and smile at her. "Everything okay?"

"How's Commodore? What did the paramedics say? Is he going to the hospital?"

"The doctor is on his way here, and he'll probably need stitches and antibiotics, but he's way too stubborn to go to the hospital."

Her expression creases with concern. "Are you sure that's the best idea?"

"It was a graze. He said he had worse in the war."

"What about . . . Mrs. Rango?" McKinley asks.

"The deputies blocked off the area, and the coroner arrived before we came inside."

"I still can't believe this . . ." Whitney trails off.

"I know. But it's not your fault."

She shakes her head as I wrap an arm around her shoulders. "I just want it all to be over. I don't want to lose anyone else. I don't care who it is. There's been too much loss."

"It will be over. I promise."

"Ricky's fans are going to be so angry when they hear about Renee," Whitney whispers.

"And that's not our problem." I close my arms around her and pull her into my chest. "It's going to be fine. I'm proud of you. You were amazing." I press a kiss to her forehead.

McKinley's cell phone rings, and she pulls it from her pocket to look at it. "I'm sorry, I have to take this. Will you excuse me?"

"We'll leave you here in peace. I'll be close if you need me, Mac."

"Don't call me that," my sister says before she answers the phone.

She starts talking, and I lead Whitney toward the door.

"I'm worried about her," Whitney says. "She puts on a good front, but she's still a little girl who just lost her mom and then saw her grandpa get shot."

My hand tightens its grip on Whitney's. "I know. But I also know my sister. She's not playing. She's strong. She'll grieve, but it'll happen in her own time and her own way."

"What about you?" she asks.

"I've been grieving the loss of my mother since the night my father died. We lost part of her then, and we never got her back."

Whitney's arms wrap around me. "I'm so sorry, Lincoln. I could apologize a million times and it wouldn't be enough. I just hope Commodore—"

I interrupt her before she can keep saying she's sorry. "It's not your fault. You didn't do any of this. I didn't do any of this. That's what we have to remember. We did nothing wrong. Please tell me you understand and believe that."

Whitney is quiet for several moments. "I'm not going to run, if that's what you're asking." She looks up at me, and the conviction in her expression gives me a punch of strength. "I'm done running. I'm staying here. With you. If you'll still have me."

"I'll always have you." I lower my forehead to hers and breathe her in as I squeeze her tighter. "You leaving is the one thing that would break me, Blue. With you, I can take on anything. Without you, I'd go back to being a shell of a man."

I pause for a beat, and I know this isn't the time to share what else I'm thinking, but if today has taught me anything, it's that there is no guarantee of tomorrow. I pull back to meet her beautiful blue gaze that sucked me in from that very first night.

"Someday soon, I'm going to ask you a really important question, Whitney, and I want you to say yes."

WHITNEY

He's going to ask me to marry him.

As I sit at the ridiculously long table in the dining room of the Riscoff estate, it takes the remaining reserve of my strength after this marathon of a day to keep my expression calm. Inside, I'm grappling with everything that has happened. *Could I have misunderstood him?*

Shivers ripple across my skin, and I don't know what to think. If Lincoln meant what I thought he meant . . . Everyone who told me he'd never want to marry me was *wrong*.

I reach for my water glass, needing to do something with my hands as we wait for Commodore to position himself at the head of the table and finally speak. His fresh shirt is snowy white beneath the navy-blue sling, and his eyes are clear despite the pain he must be in, since Lincoln told me he refused drugs other than antibiotics.

"I asked you all to have dinner with me this evening because I want to make it very clear what matters to me at this phase of my life—especially after the circus earlier—and that's family."

Commodore's serious gaze moves from McKinley and Harrison on one side of the table and to me and Lincoln on the other. His attention seems to linger even longer on me.

"She's not family," Harrison says, staring at me. "She's a Gable—"

"When I want your opinion, boy, I'll ask for it."

Harrison shuts his mouth, and I'm certain Commodore just gave him another reason to hate me more than he already does.

"Lincoln has made it clear that Whitney belongs with him, and I suspect it's only a matter of time before her status in this family is official."

"Yes, sir," Lincoln says. "You're correct."

My cheeks heat as everyone looks to me. *This is really happening. I didn't misunderstand anything about what Lincoln said.*

If you had asked me two months ago if I'd ever get married again, my answer would have been *hell no, absolutely not. No way. No how*. But Lincoln has always been the one. I gave him up once, and I've been lying to myself if I thought that I'd ever be able to do it again.

"Regardless of her last name, she's shown herself to be strong, resilient, loyal, and intelligent. Maybe with this union, the feud between our families will finally be put to rest—before any more losses are suffered on either side."

Harrison scoffs, but Lincoln raises his glass.

"I can drink to that."

Commodore nods and we all raise our glasses high, except Harrison, whose whiskey tumbler hovers near his lips.

"To the next generation. May they not be touched by the tragedy we've suffered."

We all toast to Commodore's words, and I tip back the wine in my glass.

"But what if there's already a next generation? I thought we decided that Ricky Rango already has a kid running around out there, or there's no way his crazy mom would worry about a paternity test after all this time."

Of course Harrison can't let us have one single moment of relative peace, but I can't say I haven't been wondering and worrying about the same thing.

"Unless someone else comes forward, we may never know the truth," Commodore says. "But regardless of the answer to that question, nothing changes. Lincoln will lead this family and the company after I'm gone."

"And McKinley gets the resort and I get nothing. I see how it works."

Commodore's hard stare sharpens on Harrison. "You will get what you deserve, and only your actions and effort will dictate exactly what that is."

"I already know what you've decided, old man. There's no question there." Harrison rises from the table, whiskey glass in hand. "It's always been bullshit. Enjoy your dinner. I'll be mourning the loss of my mother while I get drunk."

We all watch him as he stalks out of the room.

"I'll never understand him," McKinley says quietly.

Commodore glances at her. "That, my dear, is what entitlement looks like. He will never work for what he wants. He'll always expect it to be given. As long as that continues, he'll be given nothing."

Through the rest of dinner, the tension at the table is

thick enough to cut with a knife. Commodore tells stories about his childhood, but everyone's laughter sounds brittle and forced. After what McKinley said about her parents, I can't help but wonder if there's ever been real laughter in this house.

Maybe . . . just maybe . . . that's something I can change in the future.

I have no idea how, but I just made myself a new goal.

───────

"ARE YOU SURE ABOUT THIS?" I ask as Lincoln leads me up the grand staircase, and all I can remember is the room from a decade ago when his mother caught us together.

"You're not staying in a guest room. You're with me. Even my grandfather understands and has given his blessing—not that we needed it. Besides, after today . . . I need you close."

He pulls me into his arms, his chin brushing the top of my head. The stiffness of his posture seems to melt away as he simply holds me in the middle of the hallway.

Maybe I can give him exactly what I was seeking —peace.

We stand there for long moments, and by the time he releases me, every inch of my skin buzzes where it touches his. Despite the fact that I should be exhausted, part of me is alive and anticipating what's coming next. Lincoln never fails to send my senses into overdrive.

My brain may be caught up in everything that has happened today, but my body is already moving beyond it.

Still, when we continue down the hallway, I have to ask, "Are you sure you don't want to spend more time with your sister or your grandfather? I don't want to take you away from your family tonight."

Lincoln pauses in front of a large wooden door and drops my hand in favor of resting his palms on my shoulders. His hazel stare is serious when he speaks.

"I don't know how long it'll take you to accept it, Blue, but you're my family too. And tonight, I need you."

LINCOLN

IT'S BEEN the day from hell, and I'm raw. There's only one thing in this world that can soothe me, and that's Whitney. Her blue eyes go soft when I tell her exactly what she means to me, and her lips part.

I lower my mouth to hers, taking the smallest taste. It's not enough. With Whitney Gable, *enough* isn't a concept. I'll never tire of kissing her lips, worshipping her body, and hearing her say my name when she comes.

What I need tonight is everything that is her. I reach behind us and wrap my fingers around the handle. As soon as the door swings open, I pull her inside.

I haven't had a designated bedroom at the estate since I moved out, but on the rare occasions I've stayed here since, this is my room of choice. Of all the guest suites, it's the simplest. But tonight, all that matters is that it has a bed where I can spend the night wrapped around the woman I love.

The woman I'm going to marry.

A sense of possession rushes over me and I kick the

door shut behind us, never taking my lips from hers. The slamming echoes in the room, bouncing off the high ceiling and dark green walls, but I couldn't care less. Whitney's tantalizing scent, a sweet mix of warm vanilla and coconut, invades my senses, and I can't wait to see if her skin tastes like it smells.

I drop my hands from her hair and wrap them around her waist to pick her up and carry her to the bed. "I don't give a damn what happens tonight, we're not leaving this room. I don't care if the entire estate is burning down around—"

Whitney pulls her mouth back to press a finger against my lips. "Don't say that."

"Fair enough," I say as I press a kiss to the pad of her finger. "But I'm going to say this. I love you, Whitney Gable, and there's nothing I want more than to spend every night of the rest of my life with you."

WHITNEY

His words have the power to make me swoon.

"I love you, Lincoln."

His features soften and his eyes drift closed. "Say it again."

"I love you. I've always loved you. I will always love you."

Lincoln bows his head to rest against my forehead. "I don't deserve you. Not after everything I—"

"Don't say it." I press a kiss to his lips. "Because you're wrong."

Lincoln takes control of the kiss and presses me back against the bed. His lips skim down to my jaw and up to my ear. He pauses there.

"I'll prove it to you. I'll show you I deserve you. I'll be the man you've always needed me to be. No more letting you down. I promise you. I love you so fucking much, Blue."

"You don't need to prove anything to me. All I've ever wanted is your love."

"You have it, but that's just the beginning," Lincoln says before he turns ravenous.

He's on a mission tonight, and even if he doesn't realize it, I do. He's trying to escape the grief of what happened today, and there's nothing I won't do to help him. There's nothing I wouldn't do for him, period.

It's a simple fact now. No questions asked. Our path may never be smooth and easy to navigate, but we've been through too much in finding our way back to each other to give up again.

Lincoln Riscoff is mine.

His lips coast down my neck, leaving a wake of heat. He slips my shirt over my head, then cups my breasts in his hands.

"So beautiful. So fucking beautiful."

With a tug, Lincoln frees my breasts and thumbs my nipples. The buds tighten into even harder nubs, desperate for his mouth next. He rolls them between his thumb and forefinger, and I writhe on the bed beneath him as heat builds between my legs.

"I don't spend enough time on your gorgeous tits. That all changes now." He pinches them tighter between the pads of his fingers, and a bolt of pleasure shoots through me as I buck my hips up toward his body.

He covers one nipple with his mouth and sucks hard enough to steal a gasp from me. When he switches to the other side, the sparks of heat grow to the point where I think I might actually come from this alone. I never have before, but Lincoln has proven to be the exception to every rule.

When he scrapes across the tender skin with his teeth

and pinches the opposite nipple, something breaks inside me and a rush of pleasure sweeps through.

"Oh my God. Oh my God." I grip his shoulders hard as I ride it out.

When I finally release him, Lincoln lifts his head. "You're so beautiful. I need to see that again."

He lifts up from the bed and his fingers go to the waist of my pants. Within seconds, I'm naked but for a thong, and Lincoln presses his mouth against the lace, breathing me in.

"Please, I need . . ."

"Everything. You need fucking everything from me, and I'm going to give it to you."

When he snaps the elastic on my panties, the only barrier between us is gone.

He takes his time, licking and stroking, bringing me all the way to the edge and pushing me over again and again until I'm not sure I can hold back another scream. But he doesn't stop.

Lincoln's determined to make me beg, and if this is the way he wants to cope with his grief, there's no way in hell I'm going to stop him.

As long as the orgasms don't kill me.

LINCOLN

WHEN I FINALLY PUSH INSIDE Whitney, my balls are drawn up so tight, I'm afraid I won't last beyond the second pump. I force myself to slow down and look into her eyes. They're hazy with the remnants of her last orgasm, and her lips are curled into a feline smile.

I will never tire of that expression for as long as I live.

"I love you, Blue, and I'm going to spend the rest of my life proving to you just how much."

"I told you, you don't have anything to prove."

"I do, and I will. Just wait."

I drive into her three more times, and when her inner muscles clamp down tightly on me, I lose myself in her body.

The rest of my life won't be long enough. I need forever with this woman.

When dawn breaks, I regret the fact that I didn't pull the drapes closed last night, because the bright morning light is impossible to sleep through. My body is curled around the woman I never want to let out of my arms again. The woman who gave me solace last night when I would have otherwise sworn I wouldn't find it.

As much as I want to avoid the feelings of grief trapped inside me forever, I know I'll have to deal with them eventually. *But not yet.*

Whitney stirs and lifts her head. "So bright."

"I know. I'll close the curtains, and you keep sleeping. I'll come back to wake you up in an hour."

She must only be partially awake, because she mumbles something and tugs the blanket closer to her face. In seconds, her breathing shifts back to the even pattern I've memorized.

I wish we could rewind to the morning we were at my house, and I could leave her sleeping in my own bed, except this time I wouldn't fuck everything up by jumping to conclusions when I read the news headline.

What's done is done. The only thing I can do is move forward and prove to her that I'm not going to fuck up again. *Never again.*

I pull on a T-shirt I left in the drawer the last time I stayed here and my pants from yesterday, then leave the room quietly. When I venture downstairs, I find my grandfather and my sister both in the dining room. McKinley has her laptop next to her plate, and she works while stealing bites of toast. Commodore reads the paper as steam rises from his coffee. Both of their heads lift when I step into the room.

"Anything new this morning?"

McKinley glances up at me. "Not yet. I have an idea I want to run past you, though."

My grandfather narrows his gaze over the paper at her. "What kind of idea?"

"The kind that both of you are going to think is crazy, but I think is smart. And since I'm in charge of the resort . . ."

"What are you hinting at? Might as well just tell us," Commodore says.

"Whitney's cousin's wedding and reception is next week, and I want to empty the main wing of the hotel, the tower, so there's absolutely no chance that anything or anyone could possibly ruin her day."

"You want to cancel the reservations?" I ask, disbelief in my tone.

"Not cancel them, move them all to the garden wing. I've already written a letter to send to the guests whose rooms would be impacted. Anyone who isn't going to get the view they requested will receive a free night's stay for their next trip. Since we never run sales or specials of any kind, I don't think most will object."

My brain finally catches up to my sister's logic. "That way we could arrange security to block off access to the main tower. Close the restaurant, and only offer dinner that night in the garden to other guests."

"Exactly. Then we wouldn't have to worry about the media somehow sneaking inside, because we can practically lock down the entire hotel."

Harrison appears in the doorway. "You're going to do all that for Cricket Gable's wedding? That seems like overkill for a pot-smoking hippie."

McKinley's attention cuts to where he stands in the doorway opposite me. "It's not just for Cricket. It's for Whitney. She's family now, and we're closing ranks to keep her safe. Isn't that right, Grandfather?"

Commodore lowers his paper to the table and studies my sister. "You're going to be the one facing the guests who are inconvenienced. Are you sure that's the smartest business decision?"

"Yes," McKinley replies, showing wisdom and strength when talking about the resort. She's in her element as she continues. "Because the last thing we need is another incident, and at the end of the day, I'm the one who's in charge of making sure Whitney's cousin has the best wedding day she can imagine. And that's exactly what I'm going to give her."

"This is why I should've been in charge of the hotel." Harrison steps into the room, adding a punch of resentment to each word. "You're too damn sentimental to realize you're making a huge mistake."

Commodore looks from him to McKinley. "I approve of your decision. That's exactly what I would do." His gaze flicks back to Harrison. "And your attitude is another reason I didn't put you in charge of anything."

My brother sputters. "But you only care about the bottom line. When have you ever given a damn about anything else?"

My grandfather raises his chin. If Harrison were smart, he'd be afraid of whatever is going to come out of Commodore's mouth next.

"Protect and preserve the legacy goes far beyond business. We uphold our principles, our name, and our honor, leaving everything we touch better for the next generation than when we were given control of it."

"And now the next generation is going to be Ricky Rango's goddamn bastard kid that's out there somewhere, or one that's half fucking Gable." Harrison's tone drips disgust. "Great goddamn legacy you've got there."

Commodore's good elbow hits the table and the china rattles. "Get out of this house. Take nothing but those things you actually paid for yourself. I'll have your credit cards shut off within the hour. Let's see how you handle life in the real world without that legacy."

My brother's face morphs into a picture of rage. "You've got to be fucking kidding me."

"It's time for you to learn, boy. Your brother went off and made his mark before he came back, and we should've done the same with you, but your mother didn't want you to be away longer than you had to be."

My brother's glare skewers each of us. "I'm glad she didn't live to see the day when a Gable was welcomed into this house and her son was thrown out. *That* would've killed her."

"You're officially fired and homeless, Harrison. Get the hell out." Commodore's declaration leaves absolutely no room for misinterpretation. "Come back when you can prove that you're worthy of the Riscoff name."

"Fuck you. Fuck every single one of you." Harrison stomps out of the room, and a vase smashes to the floor as he brushes past it.

"He's going to make a mess," McKinley says as she shoves her chair back and pushes to her feet.

"Then let him. It's time for him to grow up and learn how to act like a decent human being. Whatever he destroys will be something he'll have to replace in the future."

A feeling of foreboding settles over me as I hear more glass shatter.

This isn't going to end well.

WHITNEY

THE SOUND of doors slamming and things breaking jerks me out of sleep. My body tenses as I blink and remember the crashing and banging of Ricky destroying everything in the house when I wouldn't come out of the safe room that fateful day.

My heart rate skyrockets and my breathing speeds up.

No. Ricky's dead. I'm not in the safe room.

I blink in the darkness, working to get my bearings.

I'm at the Riscoff estate. Commodore ordered us to stay here. I reach out and feel the bed. The sheets beside me are cold, and I vaguely remember Lincoln's voice earlier this morning.

Another door slams, and it sounds like the force should have been hard enough to crack it.

I pop out of bed and throw on my clothes before I rush out into the hallway. There's no war going on that I can see, but someone is definitely throwing a fit of rage. *I bet I only need one guess as to who that is . . .*

As soon as I see a suitcase being tossed into the

hallway and Harrison's furious face follow it out of a doorway, I wish I'd stayed in bed.

He straightens when he sees me, his chest heaving and nostrils flaring. "This is your fault. You couldn't keep your goddamned legs closed, and now you're fucking ruining everything."

It's still early, yet I can't help but wonder if he's already drunk, because he's not making any sense.

I know better than to embroil myself in confrontations I don't understand, so my first instinct is to pull myself back into the room and lock the door until whatever enraged Harrison Riscoff passes. But that's the old Whitney, whose first instinct is to curl into a ball and protect herself. Maybe this is the wrong time to take a stand, but something that feels a lot like confidence keeps my spine ramrod straight as I face Harrison.

"I don't have a clue what went wrong in your privileged world, but I do recognize a grown man throwing a temper tantrum when I see it."

He drops the bag he's holding and stalks toward me.

Shit. Maybe this was a bad idea.

"I hope you're happy that you're destroying this family one generation at a time. I don't know what you did to make my grandfather think you're holier-than-thou, but I guarantee it won't last. My brother is only with you because he wasn't supposed to be. Now that he's got the green light to bang your skank ass, he won't stay with you long. The appeal is gone. You're not a challenge anymore. Don't get used to being lady of the manor, because you'll be outside the gates looking in again before you know it." Harrison's glare sharpens. "I predict it won't even take a week. Enjoy it while it lasts."

He turns and marches back to his bags, and I can't help but wonder what exactly I missed this morning.

Is Harrison really leaving in protest?

Lincoln comes up the stairs as his brother drags his expensive luggage down the hall, and I have to wonder if it's the first time he's carried his own bags in his entire life.

"What? You checking to make sure I didn't take anything I wasn't supposed to? Go ahead, search my bags. See if I fucking care." Harrison spits the words like venom at his brother.

"I don't give a damn what you took. I only hope you lose the attitude."

Harrison glances at me. "I didn't want to be under the same roof as your whore anyway. Commodore thinks I can't make it on my own? He'll regret this."

Lincoln steps out of his brother's way as he heads for the stairs. "I'll text you the funeral plans. I'm sure Commodore wouldn't want you to be excluded from those."

"I don't give a damn what Commodore wants anymore. I'm not missing my mother's funeral, and he can go fuck himself if he thinks differently."

As Harrison drags his suitcases down the stairs, Lincoln stands with his back toward me, watching the bags thump from one step to the next.

As soon as he turns around, I rush toward him. "What the hell happened? Did Commodore kick him out?"

"Until further notice. He told Harrison it was time he prove he's worthy of the family name."

"That's a little harsh." I'm shocked I'm speaking up for

Harrison, considering all the hate he's spewed at me, but he did just lose his mother yesterday.

Lincoln nods. "But it might be the best thing to ever happen to him. Other than college, he's never lived anywhere else. He's never had to earn a paycheck to make sure he has a roof over his head and food on his plate."

I raise an eyebrow. "And you did?"

"From the day I graduated from college until a few days before I met you, I was cut off completely. No family money there to cushion my fall if I failed. It taught me something that Harrison desperately needs to learn—what it is to be your own man."

The front door slams and I wince. "He doesn't sound like he agrees with you."

"Doesn't matter. He'll figure it out, or he'll have to swallow his pride and come crawling back to Commodore and apologize. Enough about my brother. There's something I wanted to tell you about your cousin's wedding at the resort."

I have so many more things to say about this subject, but none of it is going to be helpful right now, so instead I smile.

"What about Cricket's wedding? Is there an issue?"

"No issue, but wait until you hear what McKinley's going to do for her."

LINCOLN

WITH RENEE RANGO'S DEATH, the exhumation of my father's body has been canceled, but part of me wonders if that was really the right choice. I can't escape the nagging feeling that maybe we should have done it anyway, but Commodore made the decision, and I'm not going to argue it right now.

The last thing we need in this family is more potential for disaster, and removing my father's casket from the mausoleum seems like an invitation for it. Besides, with Harrison in charge of security, it was going to be a clusterfuck.

The fact that Whitney and I are in the library instead of dodging press and dealing with the past is vastly preferable. I'm working through contracts as she writes, at least until her phone buzzes on the table between us.

I look at the name on the display. *Asa*.

Fuck. Whitney's brother.

I'll never forget the beating he gave me, or how he threatened to kill me the day of her wedding.

"Are you going to answer that?" I ask as she stares at the phone and then looks up at me.

"What am I going to say to him?"

"Tell him the truth."

Whitney's face pales, and there's no doubt she remembers exactly how much her brother hates me too. He probably hates me more than my brother hates her. *Obviously, our family issues are going to take some time to work out.*

She answers the phone. "Asa?"

"Where the hell are you? Where the hell is everyone?"

Even though it's not on speaker, I can hear every word, and I grimace. *He has to be here in Gable. Fuck.*

"What do you mean? Where are you?" Whitney asks, and I don't know if she's hoping he's not really here or if she hasn't put it together yet. I'm going with the former over the latter.

"I'm standing in front of Aunt Jackie's house, and there's a guy here who just told me one hell of a story about what's been going on with the family that no one else bothered to mention. Where the hell are Jackie and the twins?"

Well, that answers my question.

"Aunt Jackie, Karma, and her kids are staying at The Gables right now. Cricket is with her fiancé."

"And where are you?"

Whitney swallows, and I know she's not looking forward to breaking the news to her brother. She glances at me as she straightens in her seat.

"I'm at the Riscoff estate."

Asa doesn't answer for several moments, and when he does, his tone is tight. "Jesus fucking Christ. You better tell them to let me in, because I'm on my way."

WHITNEY

"I DON'T WANT to be here either, but you better show me where my sister is."

Asa's voice booming from the front door is impossible to miss, even though I can't see him from the entrance to the library.

"I apologize in advance if this turns into a mess," I say to Lincoln. Asa can be a loose cannon, and I can only imagine what he's going to say now.

Lincoln squeezes my hand. "He's a good brother. I can respect that."

The last time I saw Asa was in LA three days after Ricky died. The fact that he's only now showing up in Gable doesn't surprise me. Asa is often cut off from communication and news from the civilian world as part of his job.

What that job is exactly, I don't know and he won't tell me. He was only in LA for a few hours, because that's all the time he could spare from whatever he was working on. He offered me money, but I turned it down out of pride and told him Ricky left me plenty. When he finds out I lied to him, it's not going to be pretty.

Lincoln and I head for the foyer and meet Asa.

"Fucking hell, Whit. You've got a lot of goddamn explaining to do." He strides toward me and scoops me up in his arms in a hug.

"I'm sorry I didn't tell you about any of this. I figured you were way too busy."

"I'm never too busy for my family. Ever. It might take me a few days to get back to you, but it's not because I want it that way. I heard the news. What a fucking mess. There's no way Ricky was really a Riscoff. No fucking way," my brother says quietly. "I don't believe it. He never said a word. And then his mom . . ."

It's easy to forget that Asa and Ricky were friends for years, especially when my memory of Ricky has morphed into something so different.

"I'm so sorry about Renee," I tell my brother. "I know you knew her . . . before."

"She was batshit crazy from day one. Definitely crazy enough to make up a story like this. I don't think there's a chance in hell it's true, though," he says.

"Ricky might not have known."

Asa shakes his head. "Renee never could've kept it quiet this long. I don't believe it."

That's when I blurt out the secret I was keeping from him too. "Renee told me who Ricky's dad was the day Ricky proposed."

"What?" My brother's eyes widen and he glances at Lincoln for the first time, but looks immediately back at me.

81

I explain, quickly and succinctly, all the threats Renee made to force me into the wedding.

"Jesus Christ, Whit." He crushes me in another hug. "I thought you loved him. I did. I would never have pushed you into it if I didn't think it was the best thing for you. I'm so fucking sorry, Whitney. I wish you'd told me."

"I didn't want you to know. I made my choices, and I lived with them." I look up at my big brother. "Now I need you to be able to live with the choices I'm making now."

His expression darkens as he shifts his attention back to Lincoln. I expect my brother to tell me to keep dreaming, but instead he asks me a single question. "Do you love him?"

"Absolutely and completely."

"Then I'll withhold judgment. For now."

"Thank you." Lincoln finally speaks, and the fact that he stayed quiet this long and let me and my brother say what we needed to say makes me love him even more. "And you're more than welcome to spend as much time with Whitney here as you want. I'm sure there's a lot your sister would like to tell you. If you need a place to stay, we can set you up with a room on the VIP floor at The Gables."

"Are you giving away my rooms again?" McKinley says as she joins us.

"I do need to talk to my sister, but I don't need your charity. I pay my own way."

"Mr. Gable, we don't consider it charity. We consider it making sure everyone is shielded from the press to the extent we can assure it," McKinley says, countering him.

Asa's gaze narrows on her. "I can handle myself just fine, Ms. Riscoff."

McKinley shifts her weight from foot to foot, and I have to wonder if Asa makes her nervous.

"Let's take this conversation to the library," Lincoln says. "Whitney can catch you up on everything that's happened."

My brother's muscles tense, and I know he wants to spend time at the Riscoff estate about as much as he wants to step on an IED.

"Please, Asa."

LINCOLN

ASA GABLE, a man I've always thought was unflappable, looks dumbfounded when Whitney finally finishes explaining everything that has happened since she returned to Gable.

"Jesus Christ. If I'd known, I'd have left the jungle and gotten my ass here a hell of a lot sooner. This is a goddamned disaster. You shouldn't have to deal with this shit alone."

"She's not dealing with it alone. Your sister has the full power of the Riscoff family behind her."

Asa's gaze flicks to me. "She shouldn't need it. She should be able to have the quiet, simple life she wanted after Ricky died. This isn't that."

"That's not their fault, Asa. It's Ricky and Renee's," Whitney says.

"I know. I just want you to be happy, and having the press come down twice as hard on you isn't making that happen." He pauses. "And then Renee gets a gun and it all goes to hell, and now we'll never know the truth."

"Didn't she submit the DNA sample for testing anyway?" McKinley asks. "Couldn't we still pursue it?"

"No. She had forty-eight hours to provide one after a DNA sample could be collected from Father, so her sample was never delivered."

"Do you really think she had one?" Whitney's brother sounds skeptical when he voices the question.

"I don't know. Part of me says no. I think there's a good chance she just wanted money, and expected that by sending the letter to Commodore, he'd pay her off with a quick settlement to keep it all quiet."

Asa leans back in his seat and crosses his arms. "Renee always had money when we were growing up. Ricky had the best of everything, even though she didn't work. I always wondered about his dad, and thought maybe he was paying the bills, but we never talked about it."

His observation drops like a lead weight in my gut. "If we look at it logically, there's a good chance money is all she was after. If my father was paying her to keep quiet, the money would've stopped when he died."

"But by then, Ricky was starting to make money," Whitney says.

I nod. "And Renee had you to write the songs to ensure he kept making money."

"That fucking bitch," Asa whispers. "And when Ricky died . . . she needed a new income stream."

I finish his train of thought. "Which fits with the timing of Commodore getting the request for a paternity test just after Ricky died."

"Jesus fucking Christ." Asa shoots to his feet. "I wish I'd known. I never would've let her get away with this. I would've gotten answers, and now there's no goddamned chance we can."

"Unless . . ." McKinley's voice is hesitant. "Unless someone comes forward with a kid that's Ricky's."

I SHAKE MY HEAD. "I don't think there is one. If she had a grandkid she was protecting, she wouldn't have done what she did today."

"You're right." Shockingly, Asa agrees with me, and then he says something I don't expect. "Has anyone thought about exhuming Ricky's body? That's the only other way to tell."

We all look at him, and I wonder why the hell I didn't think of it first.

"Ricky was cremated. It was Renee's choice," Whitney says quietly.

"Why would she have him cremated if his DNA could possibly prove her case?" my sister asks.

"Because she's a liar and she didn't want anyone to be able to prove it," Asa says as he grips the back of his neck. "We need to find out more. Hire a PI. Get proof either way."

"We're already on it. There are several investigators currently working on the situation."

Whitney's brows go up. "There are?"

"Yes, and they'll tell us immediately if they find anything."

"Good. Keep me informed."

I don't like Asa Gable giving me orders, but in the interest of keeping the peace, I nod.

Whitney rises and moves toward her brother. "Are you staying? What's your plan?"

"I'm here until after Cricket's wedding, and then I have to get back."

"Get back where?" McKinley asks, and quite frankly, I'm shocked by her question and her curiosity about him.

"That's above your pay grade, Ms. Riscoff." He turns to look at Whitney. "I'm going to go check in on Aunt Jackie. You coming?"

"Commodore thought it would be safer if we all stayed here for now."

Her brother's gaze cuts to me. "Really? The old man has you on lockdown?"

"Your name has been added to the guest list," I tell him instead of giving him the confrontation he seems to want. "Feel free to come back anytime."

Asa nods at me, and I still see mocking derision in his gaze.

"Take care of my sister, or I'll take care of you." With that vague threat, he heads for the door.

McKinley watches him as he leaves. "He's . . . interesting."

"He's been in the military since he turned eighteen, so he's a little . . . rough," Whitney explains.

My sister stares at the door he just walked out of with enough concentration that I'm tempted to return the beating Gable gave me to encourage him to stay the hell away from her.

"He's not in uniform."

"I don't think he's active duty any more. I don't actually know what he does . . . because he'll never say."

From the look of her brother, I'm going to guess that

MEGHAN MARCH

Whitney is one hundred percent accurate. She must not have caught the ten-thousand-dollar watch he was wearing on his wrist, but I did.

I don't know what Asa Gable does, but it pays a hell of a lot better than Uncle Sam.

One more mystery to add to the unsolved column, but at least this one doesn't bother me too much. No matter what Asa thinks of me, he'll never do anything he thinks will hurt his sister.

"So, what's next on today's exciting agenda?" McKinley asks. "Because I'm not sure if I need to start drinking yet or wait until later."

WHITNEY

WITH THE PRESS still in a frenzy outside the gates due to the grisly events of a few days ago, plus my bombshell confession about Ricky, Commodore still insists we only leave the house if absolutely necessary. When I ask about my cousin's final dress fitting and he deems it unnecessary, I disagree completely.

"I appreciate your concerns," I tell him, "but this isn't something I can miss. She's not just my cousin; she's my best friend. I've already let the media take enough from me, and I'm not giving this up too."

He shifts in his power chair and studies me for a solid minute. "And if I still say no?"

"I'll leave anyway. You said it yourself—what matters most is family, and Cricket might as well be my sister."

For a few moments, I expect him to shut me down completely, but he tilts his head.

"Have them come here instead. You're right; there's no reason we should let the press keep us from important things. However, to protect our privacy, we may have to rearrange things."

There's a note of respect in his tone, and I accept the compromise.

Two hours later, I hug Cricket as she walks into the Riscoff mansion, her eyebrows nearing her hairline.

"I'm sorry for the inconvenience. But with everything happening, I was hoping you wouldn't mind too much."

Cricket releases me. "Shut up, Whit. This is awesome."

"And when we're done, we have a champagne lunch waiting for us out in the garden."

Her eyes practically bulge out of her head. "Are you serious?"

I nod. "I wanted to make today special."

"Mission accomplished. You're the best."

The seamstress arrives moments later, and we move to the conservatory where a pedestal has been set up for the final fitting.

"Are you sure you're not going to change your shoes? You don't want to wear heels to the reception?" the seamstress asks.

Cricket sticks her Birkenstock-clad foot out from under the skirt of the dress. "I'm wearing these the whole night. Before the wedding, during, and after. No one is changing my mind, and I don't care if you think they don't match."

I bite my lip to quash my grin, because the seamstress clearly doesn't know Cricket that well. It comes as zero surprise to me that she's wearing sandals on her big day. It doesn't matter that she's getting married at what is likely the most expensive venue in the state—she's still Cricket, and that's just one thing I love so much about her.

"Fine. Fine. I just wanted to give you the chance to change your mind."

Cricket crouches down so she can address the lady eye-to-eye. "I'm granola-crunchy and I like it that way. The fact that I'm wearing a traditional wedding dress at all is a miracle, and only because my mother-in-law would die if I walked down the aisle in cutoffs and a tank. Got it?"

The woman nods, and I hold back a laugh.

"You look beautiful, Cricket. The dress is perfect. Your sandals will be comfortable, and the wedding will be magical."

Tension lines my cousin's face, and some of the happiness bubbling up inside me fades when I realize she's not nearly as confident about the wedding as I am.

"I keep asking Hunter if we can just cancel the whole thing and elope. It's so much pressure, and this town has gone crazy."

Guilt floods me again because when I came back, crazy followed me to town.

"I'm so sorry, Cricket."

"No, I didn't mean because of you, Whit. You know I didn't. I keep thinking that maybe we don't need another thing to fuss over after everything that's happened."

I meet my cousin's gaze. "What do *you* want? Screw Hunter's mom and everyone else. This is *your* wedding. How do you picture it?"

She closes her eyes, and I wonder if it's the first time anyone has asked her opinion. I pray that I'm wrong.

"I want simple. Hunt and my family. Trees and mountains in the background, and the sound of rushing water underlying it all."

McKinley, who watches from the doorway, finally speaks up. "I can promise that you'll have the background and sound you want. Your family, I can't control, but we can make everything else perfect. We can cut out all the extra trappings that people usually tack on to make weddings over the top at The Gables. How about a sunset ceremony with only the people who matter to you?"

The lines on Cricket's face soften. "That sounds incredible. Like maybe there's a chance I could have a wedding that doesn't look like Bridezilla planned it."

"If that's what you want, then that's what you're going to have," McKinley says as she steps into the room. "I have the perfect spot in mind, and we'll keep it as simple as possible. Also, just so you know, we're honored to have you at The Gables for your wedding."

I already liked McKinley Riscoff, but now I like her even more because she put happy tears in my cousin's eyes.

Thank you. I mouth the words to her as the seamstress finishes the last-minute alterations on Cricket's dress.

"Do you want to join us for lunch?" Cricket asks McKinley. "I hear there's champagne."

McKinley smiles. "I'd love to."

For a few moments, I feel like everything is going to work out fine. The rehearsal is only a few days away, and then Cricket can have her beautiful but not too over-the-top wedding.

But I've been known to speak too soon.

LINCOLN

"Unfortunately, your mother's tissue didn't pass the necessary screenings for donation," the organ-donation coordinator says. "We've notified the funeral home that she is ready for pick up because the coroner has also finished, and the hospital is officially releasing—"

"What are you talking about?" I grip my phone tightly as I close myself in the room my father used as an office at the estate. "How could she not pass the screening?"

"Sir, I'm not at liberty to speak further on the subject. I'm sure the coroner would be more than happy to discuss the findings of your mother's autopsy report with you if you have questions. I know he fast-tracked it due to your family's request."

It's been three days since my mother's death, and this is the last conversation I expected to be having. I assumed all the organs and tissue had already been harvested and put into use by now. "She was on heart medication. Is that why?"

The woman clears her throat. "No, sir. That wasn't it.

You really should talk to the coroner. I can't speak further on the subject without putting my job at risk."

Frustration mounts, but I understand her position, and I know I'm not going to get anywhere if I keep pushing her.

"Thank you for the information. I'll handle it from here." I end the call, probably quicker than I should, but it's better than unleashing my temper on the messenger.

I pick up the phone to call the coroner, but when no one answers, I'm forced to leave a message full of questions.

The main one running through my mind is, *What the fuck is going on?* What could my mother possibly have been taking that would show up in a tox screening that would disqualify her from organ and tissue donation?

I leave the office and track McKinley down in the library to find out if she knows any more than I do.

McKinley shrugs. "She took heart medication. That's it, as far as I'm aware, other than vitamins. I can't imagine those would've been an issue."

"You're sure?"

"Positive," she says with a nod.

I have to believe my sister is right. I can't picture my mother being able to hide taking something. Not just because she had no way to obtain illicit drugs, but because her behavior and attitude never changed. I would have noticed.

For the first time since Harrison walked out the door, I wish my brother hadn't left. He spent more time with our mother than either McKinley or me . . . and if she wanted something, he would have found a way to get it for her.

But my brother wouldn't have acted as my mother's drug dealer. Would he?

The fact that I can't answer that question with complete certainty bothers me more than anything.

"Call Harrison. Ask him what he knows. He'll respond better to you than to me," I tell my sister.

She nods and pulls out her phone to initiate the call, but it doesn't ring. Instead, we hear a recorded message stating that his number is no longer in service.

"Fuck. Commodore already shut it down." I stare out the window for a beat before I look back at her. "Do you have any idea where he'd go?"

"Other than old frat brothers, I don't think Harrison has many friends. I have absolutely no idea who he'd call for help or where he'd go." McKinley shakes her head. "Do we know how much money he had?"

"I didn't keep track of what he kept in his bank account. He got paid well and didn't have any bills that I know of, so unless he blew it all, he would have plenty. He could be on the other side of the world by now."

McKinley presses her lips together. "I'll start looking online."

"Let me know if you find anything. I'm going to go talk to Commodore. We need the coroner to get out here and explain what the fuck is going on, because something doesn't feel right."

"THANK YOU FOR COMING, Dr. Bard. We appreciate it." I lead the coroner through the house to the office where Commodore is waiting.

"No problem at all. I'm still writing my report, so I can't give you all the details, but I've made notes so—"

"Sit down, Bard," Commodore says, interrupting the coroner. "What the hell is going on here, and why didn't you come to us directly instead of giving the transplant coordinator information that could be damaging to my family?"

I look skyward, wishing that Commodore wouldn't put our guest on the defensive before he has a chance to tell us a goddamned thing.

"Well, I . . . You know . . ."

I intervene, calming Bard's flustered nerves and sputtered words. "We understand that your first responsibility is to make sure you follow protocol, Dr. Bard. Please excuse my grandfather; he's very upset about my mother's death, and we all want to understand exactly what's going on here. My mother would've wanted to help as many people as possible with her passing, and we're confused about what could have possibly prevented her tissue from being acceptable." I may be laying it on thick about my mother, but Bard doesn't need to know the truth.

The coroner's posture relaxes after my explanation, but his worried gaze still cuts to Commodore, like he's expecting the royal inquisition.

"Why don't you have a seat, Dr. Bard. Can I get you a drink?" I ask.

"I'm still technically on the clock, so I shouldn't."

"If you change your mind, let me know. Sometimes a little Scotch goes a long way to making the end of the day bearable."

His shoulders lift to around his ears, and just as I expect, he relents. "Maybe just a splash."

Commodore sits stone-faced behind the desk as I pour and then take the seat beside Dr. Bard. It feels a little like good cop/bad cop, but then again, that's life with my grandfather.

"Why don't we cut to the chase, Bard," Commodore says. "What was in Sylvia's system that made her tissue bad?"

"It wasn't bad, per se," Bard says.

"What my grandfather means to ask is, what exactly prevented it from being acceptable to donate?" I clarify his question, sliding into my good-cop role.

Bard takes a sip of the Scotch. "If there's any chance that someone is using illicit drugs or had some kind of opiate addiction, we automatically disqualify them. We've had some issues in the past, and it's one of our bright-line rules now."

"Drug user? Opiate addict? My mother?" Shock permeates my tone. "What the hell would make you think that?" *And the good-cop portion of this session is over.*

"We found evidence of a highly addictive painkiller in her bloodstream that was never prescribed to her, according to the medical records we reviewed."

I can't for the life of me picture my mother popping pills, but then I remember my conversation with McKinley. If my mother had any kind of drug problem, Harrison would know, and we still haven't been able to track him down.

"What did you find?" I ask, my tone demanding.

"Fentanyl."

"What?" Commodore asks. "Where would she get it?"

"I was worried about this." Bard looks at me and then my grandfather, his expression concerned. The glass of Scotch dangles in his hand. "You didn't know. And . . ."

"What?" I snap.

"From the hospital chart, I understand it was assumed that Mrs. Riscoff died of a heart attack."

"Yes, that's correct," I say.

The coroner slides the glass onto the desk and sits straighter in his chair. "The hospital was incorrect. Based on the tox screen, her cause of death was an overdose."

My heart pounds in my ears. "An overdose? On fentanyl?"

The coroner nods, and I drop my head into my hands. *Holy fucking hell. This can't be happening.*

I lift my chin and meet Bard's gaze. "Is there any possibility it wasn't an overdose?"

Bard shakes his head. "No. None at all. That's the official cause of death."

"But is there a chance it wasn't self-inflicted? Could someone else have given the drug to her without her knowledge?"

Bard's bushy eyebrows dive together. "I suppose . . . that could be possible, even though in my experience, it's highly unlikely. I know families don't want to think that their loved ones could have been hiding this kind of behavior, but—"

"But there's a chance my mother was murdered. Isn't that right?"

The coroner meets my gaze, his face pale. "Yes, Mr. Riscoff. Even though it's not probable, it is *possible*."

WHITNEY

LINCOLN COMES into the library where I'm writing and McKinley is working, and he looks like he's gone ten rounds with the champ in the last few hours.

I bolt out of the window seat I've taken over, sending papers flying, and rush across the room to him. "What's wrong?"

His haggard expression leads me to come to only one conclusion. *Something awful has happened.*

"What happened?" McKinley asks, rising from her laptop.

When I reach him, he wraps one arm around me and squeezes tight. Over my shoulder, he looks at his sister.

"I don't know how to tell you this, so I'm just going to say it. There's a chance that Mother was murdered."

My heart drops to the intricate rug covering the floor, and McKinley's gasp echoes from the high ceilings.

"Murdered? No. That's not possible. How could that be possible? Who? Why?"

Lincoln holds out his other arm and his sister comes

toward him, walking slowly, like her brain isn't functioning completely right.

She shakes her head. "No. No. That's not possible."

"We don't know anything for sure yet, except the fact that it wasn't a heart attack. It was an overdose of fentanyl."

"Fentanyl?" I stiffen in Lincoln's hold. "Are you sure?"

He nods gravely. "Why?"

"Because that's how Ricky died."

Lincoln's arm falls away from where he was cradling me against his chest. "Fuck. I forgot."

McKinley's mouth drops open as she meets my gaze. "I thought he died of a heroin overdose."

"Heroin mixed with fentanyl. When he was in rehab, I learned that it was fairly common for people to use both, but fentanyl is so much more potent and deadly. And it's legal if you have a prescription, which is absolutely mind-blowing."

"This seems like a hell of a coincidence." Commodore's deep voice comes from behind us as his power chair rolls into the room.

I turn to face the old man. His dark gaze is as hard as granite, and his expression says I'm the enemy again. Fear that Ricky could take this from me too, just because he couldn't control himself around drugs, rips through my system. I stiffen and stare down the Riscoff patriarch.

"I didn't kill my husband, if that's what you're asking. I wasn't there. I never saw the drugs, never touched them. There was literally no way in hell for me to make that happen. I didn't have anything to do with Sylvia's death either. I swear to God."

He leans back in his chair, his good arm crossed over his sling as he studies me. I don't know what he's looking for, but I'm equally afraid he will and won't find it.

Lincoln turns to face his grandfather. "What the hell are you getting at?"

"I might be an old man, but even I can see that two overdoses with the same drug, this close together and with people who have connections in common, doesn't seem like an accident. Sylvia was murdered, and I'm willing to put money on it that the same person might have killed them both."

"I didn't kill either of them." My tone holds all the righteous determination I can muster.

"Do you have proof?"

LINCOLN

M<small>Y</small> <small>JAW CLENCHES</small> as my grandfather stares Whitney down. I'm proud to see her holding strong, but she shouldn't have to be strong. Especially not here, where she should feel safe and protected. I'm not going to let anyone, including my own family, attack her ever again.

"She doesn't need proof, Commodore. She didn't do it, so back the fuck off."

My grandfather drops his good arm and uses it to maneuver his chair to face me. "Are you willing to bet everything on that? On her?"

I take a step toward him. "Absolutely."

The silence in the room is deafening as I wait for Commodore to make his pronouncement. But it doesn't matter what he says . . . I will stand by Whitney, whether it's in this house or as we walk away together from everything I've ever known.

"Good. I'm glad you have no doubts. And for the record, I wasn't accusing her."

"Then what the hell was that?" I ask as Commodore smiles.

"Enlightening. Now we need to figure out who the hell could have done this, or if Sylvia was much better at hiding things than any of us thought."

"WHAT DO YOU MEAN, the lawyer said he doesn't know if Mrs. Rango had a grandchild? Shouldn't he have asked his client whose paternity they were trying to establish?" I pull my phone away from my ear and stare at it for a moment like I don't understand the language the private investigator is speaking. "How could the lawyer even file the suit without knowing something like that?"

The investigator laughs. "If you saw this guy's office, you wouldn't be surprised. He's got a fancy address, but it's a closet, and I'm not even sure he passed the bar exam. He's as big of a shyster as the lawyer who never filed the divorce papers for your dad. I'll keep digging, though."

The reminder that my father couldn't even manage to hire a lawyer who would actually follow through on filing for divorce leaves a bad taste in my mouth. *How the hell could he have been so stupid?* My tone is harsher than it should be when I reply.

"Do not fuck this up. Chase every lead. If there's a chance there is a child out there, we need to know."

"Yes, sir. If the kid exists, I'll find him or her."

I end the call and immediately go looking for my grandfather.

After Bard delivered the news about the overdose, Commodore put Whitney and me on the defensive and then retired to the smoking room for a drink and a cigar. I turned down his offer in favor of not smelling like an ashtray when I finally get a chance to have dinner with Whitney later. A dinner the kitchen is preparing for us to be served in—I glance at my watch—exactly three hours.

I open the door to the smoking room and step inside. Commodore has an old leather photo album open on the table in front of him.

"May I come in?"

He looks up. "By all means."

As I move closer, I get a better look at the picture my grandfather had been staring at. It's one I don't remember. In it, Commodore looked to be about my father's age when he died, and my father was still young and gangly. He looked a lot like I did at that age, which is a sobering thought.

"Reminiscing?"

"Wondering how the hell it all went so wrong," he replies with a puff of smoke. "I should've been a better father. Maybe none of this would have ever happened if I'd been different."

Hearing Commodore sound anything other than completely confident throws me off-balance.

"I don't know how you were when my father was growing up, but I know how you were with me. I wouldn't be the man I am today without your guidance, because I sure as hell didn't follow my father's example."

Commodore lifts his gaze to mine, and for the first time, he looks all of his ninety years. "I'd like to think I learned the second time around. I knew Roosevelt wouldn't be the father he needed to be."

"As much as I don't want to bring this up right now, sir, we have another problem."

Commodore takes a long draw on the cigar and exhales smoke rings. "Bring it on, boy. None of this has killed me yet, so it's unlikely whatever you've got to say will."

"Our investigator has determined that Renee Rango never told her lawyer if there was a child when she had him start pursuing the paternity test. He assumed, but there's absolutely no proof that a child actually exists. And since Ricky Rango was cremated, we may never know for sure now if he was a Riscoff."

Commodore's fist clenches around the cigar before it comes down on the wooden table with a *thwack* hard enough to make the leather photo album jump.

"I fucking knew it. *That* is why I didn't settle. She was after the money and didn't have a damned shred of evidence to prove she deserved it." My grandfather shakes his head as he raises the cigar back to his mouth. He clamps his teeth around it, and to my surprise, he smiles. "She doesn't have jack shit. That boy wasn't your father's son, and there's no kid either. I knew it."

"Then why did you even consider exhuming my father's body?"

Commodore's self-satisfied smile widens and the cigar hangs over his lip. "I was going to call her bluff. Now we don't need to."

WHITNEY

WHEN LINCOLN COMES to our room, he looks like he's returning from fighting a war, not spending the day at his luxurious family estate.

"What happened now? Was there something else?"

He shakes his head. "No, but from what the investigator says, it's pretty clear that Renee Rango was full of it. There's no evidence Ricky ever had a kid. She dragged all of us through this for nothing."

Of course she did. And she might have lied to me about Ricky being a Riscoff too. I let her threaten me and take away ten years of the life I wanted all because she was after money. Part of me is relieved that it might finally be over, but the other part . . . the other part is *done*.

"All this destruction and loss just for *money*?" I sit on the bed, lift my knees to my chest, and wrap my arms around them. I'm officially losing it, because tears I didn't know were forming spout from my eyes and track down my face. "How dare she?"

Lincoln sits on the bed beside me and pulls me into his

lap. "I'm so sorry, Blue. So fucking sorry. You wanted peace, and you haven't found any since you came home. I promise this is all going to be over soon."

I lean against him, tears falling for all the lives that have been lost so senselessly. "It's not about me. It's about everyone. She ruined so many lives . . . all for *money*. It's disgusting." A hurricane of emotions threatens to drag me under, and there's only one way I know how to stop it. "I know you made dinner plans, but . . ."

Lincoln's hazel gaze meets mine. "Just tell me what you need. Dinner can wait."

"I need to get it all out." My fingers flex, and he knows exactly what I mean.

"I'll get you paper and pencils. And I'll be here when you're done."

He presses a kiss to my forehead, and I wrap my arms around him and hug tight.

"I don't know what else to do," I whisper. "But I have to do something before it sucks me back under."

"I know, Blue. You have your words, and I have you. I think it's fair. I'll be right back."

LINCOLN BRINGS me a blank notebook and four pencils, and then leaves the room with the promise that he won't go far.

I lose track of time writing lines about how I feel. The storm raging in this town. The secrets, the lies, the death and pain. I have to purge it from me, like it's some kind of toxin infecting my bloodstream more every second I don't put the feelings down on paper.

Every page I flip, I feel a small measure of calm return, and my hand trembles a little less.

When my fingers cramp and my wrist aches, I lay the last pencil down and can finally breathe again. I inhale slowly and let the breath out.

No matter what happens, we will be fine. I repeat the mantra over and over.

Nothing can tear us apart. Not now. Lincoln and I are stronger together than we are apart, and I'm not the Whitney Gable who runs and hides.

Not anymore.

Now I'm the Whitney Gable who stands beside the man she loves and fights when the world tries to break us.

With that vow in my mind, I leave the room to find Lincoln sitting outside the door.

"You really didn't go far, did you?"

"I'll never go further from you than I have to."

I hold out my hand, and he rises.

"I love you, Whitney. Promise me—"

I press a finger to his lips. "You don't even need to ask. I swear that no matter what comes next, you and I are rock solid. I'm done running. I know where I belong, and that's with you."

His eyes close as he whispers, "Thank you, God." And he crushes me to his chest. "We're not going to make it to dinner."

Lincoln pushes open the door of the bedroom that I just exited, and together we stumble back inside. He kicks the door shut. We strip each other naked like two crazy people, and there's only one thought on my mind.

"I need you now. Right now. Fast. Hard."

"Whatever you need, I got you." Lincoln grips my hips

and lifts me so my legs wrap around his hips. He backs me up until my spine touches the wall. "This is gonna be rough."

"I don't care. That's what I want."

With my body pinned between his hips and the wall-covering, Lincoln sweeps his thumb over my lower lips to find me soaked.

"How?" He lifts his gaze to mine.

"The last song I wrote . . . it was about us."

"And it made you wet?"

I nod.

"I don't know what I did to deserve you in my life, but I'm not going to ask questions. Not now."

"Good, because I'm done talking."

Lincoln's done talking too. He positions his cock at my entrance, and I grip his shoulders tighter as he plunges inside me with a single stroke.

I moan as my body stretches to take him. Exquisite pleasure mixed with the slightest burn of pain. It feels so perfect, and reminds of me of the most important things . . .

I'm alive, and this man is mine.

LINCOLN

OVER AND OVER, I plunge into Whitney's slick, tight pussy, and I know I'm home. I stretch, reaching down to tap her clit with my thumb, and her muscles tense before they ripple with an orgasm, clenching around my cock until I almost succumb.

But I'm not ready yet. With this woman, I'm never ready. I never want to pull away and leave her. I want to spend the rest of my life and beyond wrapped in her arms, because that's where I'm the happiest I've ever been.

Whitney Gable is the only woman I'll ever love. I've known that for a decade, even if I couldn't admit it to myself.

"I love you so much, Blue. Always."

Her blue eyes are hazy when she replies. "Always."

I thrust harder and deeper, waiting for her body to give me the signal again, and I don't have to wait long. Her pussy clamps down on me like a vise, and I'm lost.

My roar is loud enough to bring down the house, and I don't care at all who hears me.

This woman is mine.

I LOSE track of how long we've been in the room, until I hear Whitney's stomach grumble.

"You need food."

She rolls over in bed beside me, her hair mussed and cheeks pink. "I don't want to go back to reality yet."

I know what she's thinking. If we can just stay in this room, maybe we can avoid the shitstorm raging outside these walls. As much as I wish that were the case, we can't hide for long.

"Your cousin would be sad if you missed her wedding."

Whitney gives me a lopsided smile. "I guess that means we go foraging for food, and then what?"

"Figure out what's next."

I don't have to say it, but the list of what's next is long —find out if my mother took the fentanyl herself or whether someone else gave it to her, figure out where the hell my brother went, sort out the details of my mother's funeral, and make sure the media stays far away from Cricket and Hunter's wedding so that Whitney smiles on her cousin's wedding day.

And it will all be done.

I hold out a hand to Whitney and help her out of the bed. As soon as the sheet drops away from her body, my dick perks up, telling me he can find a second wind.

Whitney's gaze drops to my cock. "Are you sure you want to leave just yet? Because I can wait to eat . . ."

WHITNEY

AN HOUR LATER, my grumbling belly forces us to go in search of food. I would have thought that the kitchen of the Riscoff estate was the last place I might witness a potential murder, but Lincoln and Commodore's raised voices fill the massive space until I'm afraid my eardrums may burst.

I back away, sandwich in hand, as they argue about Sylvia Riscoff's funeral.

"No service. I stand by my decision." Commodore makes the declaration like the discussion is over, but Lincoln isn't backing down.

"That's not happening. We need closure. All of us. You're not taking that away."

Commodore leans back in his chair. "You really think a funeral is going to give you closure when we don't even know if she was a junkie who killed herself or if someone killed her? Do you want to take the chance that her murderer is at the service?"

Both Commodore and Lincoln go quiet for a beat, and that's when I realize what they're both missing.

"Isn't that why you *should* have a service? To try and draw her killer out, if there is one?"

The men look at me, and Commodore's mouth moves but no sound comes out.

Lincoln frowns. "Whitney's right. If there's a chance . . ."

"If she was murdered, then we all know the person who did it," Commodore says. "This isn't a detective show on TV. There will be no service until we know the truth. Besides, Harrison hasn't made contact, and we have no way to reach him. Do you really want your brother to miss it?"

"He wouldn't miss it if we had a way to contact him, but you had his phone shut off immediately," Lincoln shoots back at Commodore.

The old man narrows his gaze. "And I'd do it again. So we wait. We put out the word that the service is being delayed until family members can travel for it, which isn't unusual when there's a cremation, and that's the end of this matter."

Lincoln draws in a deep breath. I know he wants to argue with his grandfather, but it's not going to do any good. The old man has a will of iron, much like his grandson, and there's no changing his mind.

"I know my mother wanted to be cremated, but I think you're making a mistake, old man. But we'll do it your way—only because Harrison would never forgive any of us if he missed it."

"Good. Better to focus on the wedding this weekend. We don't need another funeral in this family right now, anyway."

WHITNEY

THE MORNING of the rehearsal dinner dawns with a raging thunderstorm over the river. I pull up the weather forecast and pray that Cricket's wedding day isn't going to be ruined by weather, even though I know that would be the top of the list of *things that don't really matter in the long run.* But still, for my cousin, I want everything to be perfect.

McKinley has already cleared the guests from the tower at The Gables, and Lincoln and I are in an SUV with Commodore's personal driver at the wheel, on our way to meet Jackie and Karma and Cricket. Or at least, I'm on *my* way to meet them. Lincoln will wait downstairs to give us time alone, and Asa texted and said he'll be coming a little later.

After not seeing my family for a few days, and after experiencing so much upheaval, I'm more eager than ever to hug them all hard. Well, Jackie and Cricket and Asa, at least.

Something has been nagging me ever since Lincoln

told me what the coroner said about his mother. I can't stop thinking that it's too coincidental that both she and Ricky essentially had the same cause of death. Granted, there was no heroin in Sylvia's tox screen, and I have a hard time attributing that kind of behavior with her. But then again, addiction isn't always obvious. People are so much better at hiding things than one would think.

With Ricky, the autopsy results weren't as much of a surprise. He had shot heroin with fentanyl before, which is what landed him in rehab. In Hollywood, a fentanyl over-dose isn't exactly a groundbreaking autopsy discovery, which is sad on a completely different level.

My thoughts go back to Sylvia as Lincoln's fingers tighten around my hand. His mother's behavior was erratic and irrational. She had mood swings. Sometimes I thought she was actually crazy. Those were all behaviors Ricky displayed when he was using, but they also seemed like part of Sylvia's normal personality.

When we pull up to the gates of The Gables, I'm happy to see the number of reporters has dwindled to a few die-hards. Since I said my piece, the tone of the stories has changed, and so has the villain. Spoiler alert, it's not me anymore. Regardless, if I never see another headline that involves me or the people I love for the rest of my life, that would be fabulous.

As hopeful optimism blooms in my chest, we pull under the overhang and one of the valets opens the back door of the SUV.

"Mr. Riscoff, Ms. Gable. We've been awaiting your arrival."

Lincoln helps me out of the SUV and hands off my bag to a bellhop. "Take good care of her," he says before pressing a kiss to my lips. "I'll be down here, waiting for you whenever you're ready."

"Thank you. Thank you so much for all of this, from me and my entire family."

He smiles. "McKinley's the one you should be thanking."

"You can say that, but I know you're the one who set it all in motion. I'll never forget that, Lincoln."

He cups my cheek. "You still don't get it. There's nothing I wouldn't do for you. But don't worry, I'll keep showing you until you believe me." He presses another kiss to my forehead. "Now go. Your family's waiting."

I rise up on my toes to kiss him again. "I love you, Lincoln Riscoff," I whisper.

His answering smile is everything I need to see as I follow the bellhop to where he's holding the elevator door open—the same elevator I once rode in and asked Lincoln if he was taking me to the dungeon. As the gold doors slide closed, I can't help but think it's crazy how much has changed since that day. It hasn't been that long, but it feels like a lifetime.

Even then, when I was pretending to hate him, I never could. I was terrified of what he might be able to do to my heart, but even that couldn't stop me from falling in love with him again. I have no defenses when it comes to Lincoln.

When we reach the VIP level, my gaze locks on the table where I last saw Sylvia Riscoff. She was having breakfast with Maren Higgins when Lincoln and I emerged from my room to take a helicopter to Blue House.

Wait a goddamned second . . . Why has no one asked Maren what the hell happened?

116

Or have they?

If Sylvia wasn't using, could someone have drugged her? Maren was right there. She had the opportunity. I don't know about means or motive, but maybe we're not looking at all the possibilities.

Part of me wants to run back downstairs to tell Lincoln, but I know I need to see my cousin right now.

"Ma'am, would you like a drink?" the bellhop asks me as I stand stock-still at the bar. "I can have anything you'd like brought to the suite."

His question snaps me out of my thoughts. "No. That's fine. I'm sorry. Just absentminded today."

I follow him to Aunt Jackie's room, and he knocks on the door. "Ms. Gable? Ms. Gable has arrived."

The door swings open, and Cricket's bright smile greets me, quieting my overactive brain. Maren can wait. This weekend is about my cousin and her happiness.

"You're here! Now the party can start!" Cricket throws her arms around me and drags me into the room. "I've missed you so much, even though it's only been a few days. How is it being locked in at the estate? I've been meaning to ask if you found any cool secret hidden rooms or moving bookshelves?"

Of course Cricket will always be the one to make me laugh, and I'm here to return the favor. I want to see nothing but smiles on her face tonight and tomorrow.

"No secret rooms or passageways, but I'm still looking."

"Snooping around the mansion. That sounds smart, Whit," Karma says, and I look over Cricket's shoulder to see her on the couch, braiding Addy's hair.

"Ignore her. I have champagne."

"Which you've had plenty of already," Aunt Jackie says, lifting the bottle out of the ice before Cricket can grab it.

"It's my wedding, and if I want to show up a tiny bit tipsy for the festivities tonight, there shouldn't be a law against that."

"Maybe your mom's right," I say. "Hold off now and have your drinks at dinner."

Cricket sighs. "Fine. But I still think it's absolutely ridiculous that I have to stay here tonight and I can't go home with Hunt. It's not like not sleeping in the same bed for one night is going to change a damn thing about the wedding."

"It's tradition," Jackie says.

"You never got married, Mom. I feel like your opinion doesn't count."

Jackie goes quiet, and a thought hits me.

Oh, Lord in heaven, please tell me that Jackie didn't have a secret wedding like Renee Rango.

Chills ripple over my skin, and I feel like someone walked over my grave.

No. It's not possible. Jackie would never have been so stupid as to do something like that and not tell anyone . . . *right?*

I remember overhearing her when I was younger, telling my mom not to ask questions about Cricket and Karma's dad. I always assumed it was a one-night stand and she didn't want to talk about it.

But what if . . .

No. I'm not going to think about it. Not tonight.

"Why don't you have a glass of champagne, Whit," Jackie says with a smile once again pasted on her face.

"You look like you could use a drink." There's something in my aunt's tone that I can't place.

Cricket whirls around. "What's going on? Did I miss something?"

Jackie walks toward her. "Of course not." She reaches out and adjusts a tendril of Cricket's hair. "You look beautiful, and tonight and tomorrow are all about *you*. It's time to live your fairy tale, my darling girl. I'm so happy for you."

I sip my champagne, putting on a happy face of my own—something I have lots of practice with—as my imagination runs away with me while Cricket puts on her short white dress for the rehearsal.

Is there something you're not saying, Jackie? And could Maren have somehow tried to frame me for Sylvia's death? Maybe she knew about Ricky's overdose and . . .

Someone knocks on the door, pulling my thoughts away from my wild theories, and I walk over to open it.

"Asa!"

My brother's broad-shouldered form fills the doorway, almost completely blocking my view of McKinley Riscoff, who must have escorted him up. Asa steps inside and lifts me in one of his fabulous hugs.

"I thought I'd have to break into the tower or scale the balconies to get to you with the security they've got here. Luckily, someone saved me from going to the trouble."

When he sets me on my feet, I peek around him to McKinley. "Thank you so much for everything you've done. We know how much it has to have inconvenienced you, and it means the world to me and my family."

She smiles, and her cheeks appear pink. *Oh Lord, what did Asa say to her?*

"It's not a problem at all. When you're ready, we've set up the rehearsal on the covered patio, since the outdoor area we planned to use is currently being pelted with rain. All you have to do is call your majordomo, and he'll escort you down."

"Thank you, McKinley. We owe you."

"Only you could say that with a straight face," Karma says with a harsh laugh.

My smile freezes as McKinley leaves the room. When she's gone, I spin around and look over to where my cousin has finished doing her daughters' hair. With the kids present, I can't say what I want to say.

Instead, I settle for, "I'm so glad we're all on our best behavior to make Cricket's wedding as wonderful as it can be." I scan all the faces in the room and find Asa staring at Karma.

He doesn't pull any punches. "Might want to reel in that attitude before you embarrass your sister, Karma."

Karma rolls her eyes. "Save it. You're barely ever here, and you don't know shit about shit."

My brother's posture stays stiff, and I'm almost worried that we're going to have a face-off between him and my cousin.

Jackie steps between them. "Enough, all of you. This is about Cricket. Let's go act like we've got some manners and sense."

I scan the room and find Cricket missing. I slip into the bedroom to find her sitting on the edge of the bed.

"Are you okay?" I ask as I sit beside her.

"I'm nervous. I hate being nervous. I'm afraid I'm going to do something wrong. Or Karma's going to say something, and then Mrs. Havalin is going to tear me apart for making her look bad."

I remember what Aunt Jackie said when I first got home—that Cricket needs backup against her future mother-in-law. Since I still haven't seen her, I've forgotten.

"I'll manage Mrs. Havalin. You worry about enjoying yourself and being in love. No one is allowed to ruin this for you. *No one.*"

Cricket gives me a weak smile. "I wish we would've eloped."

LINCOLN

THE PATIO where the rehearsal is supposed to take place is unusable. The best man's flight was delayed due to weather. And now I'm bracing for whatever else might be coming next, and praying we don't have a runaway-bride situation on our hands, because that would be about as bad as it could get.

But this is Cricket we're talking about. She and Hunter are crazy about each other. There's no way that could happen.

My faith is rewarded when Cricket, Jackie, Whitney, Karma, and Asa Gable all follow a majordomo into the rehearsal area.

Hunter strides over to Cricket. "You look beautiful," he tells her, and a little of the stiffness disappears out of Cricket's posture.

Whitney stands protectively near her cousin, and I move across the room toward them as Hunter presses a kiss to his bride's pale forehead.

"Everything okay?" I ask Whitney quietly.

"I hope so," she replies, and her response doesn't fill me with confidence.

Hunter breaks the news about the best man to Cricket.

"What are we going to do?" she asks, looking around the room, her lips pinched.

"Lincoln said he'd stand in, if we don't mind."

Cricket's worried face turns my way.

"Or you can have Asa stand in," I tell her. "Whatever you want to do, Cricket. It's your choice. We just want to make this as easy for you as possible."

Whitney squeezes my hand with approval.

"Asa's going to walk me down the aisle, so thank you," Cricket says. "We'd appreciate you standing up for us tonight."

The wedding organizer waves us over, and I return Whitney's squeeze, holding her hand tightly in my grip before I join Hunter.

When it's Whitney's turn to walk up the aisle as maid of honor, I can't help but think about the question I told her I'll be asking soon.

The ring is in the safe at the estate, and as soon as the time is right—after this wedding is finished—I'll ask the question and slide it on her finger.

Whitney gave up too much by letting Renee Rango bully her, and I'm not going to let anyone steal another minute of our future together. *Not again.*

WALKING down the aisle to Lincoln feels surreal.

Someday soon, if I know him, I'll be doing this again . . . but for real.

Instead of terrifying me, the thought fills me with strength. I've let the world chew me up and spit me out, but now I'm strong enough to fight for what I want—and what I want is this man by my side for the rest of my life.

When I reach the front of the room, I take my place off to the side near Karma.

Everything's moving smoothly until it's Asa and Cricket's turn to walk up the aisle. As soon as they take their first step, Mrs. Havalin bustles into the aisle.

"You're not waiting long enough. I told you to wait two minutes."

"Mom," Hunter says quietly from the front of the room.

"I can't help it if she doesn't know how to follow instructions. Did you tell her not to get high before the rehearsal?"

"Mother!" This time, Hunter's tone snaps like a whip. "Enough."

Cricket's face pales, and I grit my teeth. She and Asa stay where they are for another few seconds before moving forward, and I know that Mrs. Havalin and I will need to have words tonight.

Especially when she sees Cricket isn't carrying anything when she gets to Hunter.

"Where is the bouquet? There was a broach bouquet from my niece's wedding you're supposed to be carrying. Did you lose it already, Cricket? I swear, you can't do anything right."

The music goes quiet, and everyone shifts awkwardly where they stand.

"Mother, if you—"

Cricket interrupts him. "I didn't lose it, Mrs. Havalin. I told you I didn't want to use it."

"And this is all about you?" Mrs. Havalin asks.

Jackie bristles in the row across from her, her mouth opening like she's about to rain down hell on Mrs. Havalin.

I step toward Hunter's mother before she can speak. "If Cricket didn't want to use it, she doesn't have to. After all, it's just a rehearsal bouquet. Not exactly a big deal. Aren't weddings all about the bride anyway, Mrs. Havalin?"

"Maybe if they're paying for it." She narrows her eyes.

Lincoln moves to stand beside me, blocking Hunter, who looks like he's about to lose his goddamn mind. "The Gables is covering the cost of the wedding and reception, which means the bride can do and have whatever she wants."

Mrs. Havalin recoils at Lincoln's statement, and I'm thankful that he's able to intimidate her into shutting up.

Asa moves into the row next to Jackie, making me thankful that someone's there to hold her back if Mrs. Havalin speaks up again. Luckily, her mouth has been frozen in a tight smile since Lincoln's pointed remark.

The rest of the rehearsal moves along smoothly, despite Mrs. Havalin's sour face and crappy attitude, and I hope that means that the rest of the night will be easy and fun. And it is.

At least . . . until we get to the rehearsal dinner.

"I KNEW YOU WERE THE ONE," Hunter says as part of his toast. "Even if you did make me wait five years for our second date."

Everyone starts laughing, but beside me, Cricket tenses and whispers a question to me out of the side of her mouth. "What is he talking about? Five years?"

On my other side, Karma's laughter grows louder and harsher, and the hair at the nape of my neck stands on end. *Oh sweet Jesus. What now?*

Cricket leans forward and looks over me to Karma at the same moment I do. Karma covers her mouth with her hand, practically choking on her mirth. Hunter goes quiet, and everyone in the room follows suit. Every bit of attention shifts to Karma as she rocks back and forth in her chair, cackling.

Oh. My. God. A thought hits me, and it's the last thing in the world I want to be thinking. *No, she didn't.*

Cricket bolts up out of her seat, all semblance of

patience gone. "Karma, tell me right now what the hell you did."

The rest of the guests, mostly members of the Havalin family, begin to murmur, and Hunter stands beside Cricket.

"Baby, what's wrong?"

Cricket looks up at her fiancé. "I didn't make you wait five years for a second date, Hunter. That was our *first* date."

Hunter's face pales as he realizes what she's saying. "What the fuck? Then—" His gaze darts to Karma.

Tears stream down Karma's face as she continues to snort-laugh. "This is too perfect. I couldn't have planned it better myself."

"What the fuck are you talking about?" Cricket demands.

Aunt Jackie rises next. "Karma, what's going on?" She keeps her tone even, but it's clear she's concerned and jumping to the same conclusion we all are.

"It wasn't totally my fault. He just assumed . . . so I went with it."

Oh. My. God.

"You pretended to be me? With my fiancé?" Cricket screeches.

"He wasn't your fiancé then! He was drunk; we were at the bar. One thing led to another, and . . ."

Cricket spins around to face Hunter. "Please tell me she's lying. Please tell me this isn't happening. Please tell me *anything* but this."

"She answered to your name. I thought—"

"Oh. My. God." Mrs. Havalin jumps out of her chair. "Of course this would happen. I told you not to marry that girl! She and her family are trash."

"Not another word out of you." Hunter's father grabs his wife by the arm and hustles her out of the room.

The rest of us are all left staring at each other, and I pinch the inside of my elbow. It stings like hell, so I know I'm not having a nightmare. *But I wish I was.*

"I can't believe this. I . . . I . . ." Tears trickle down Cricket's cheeks, and as I wrap my arms around my cousin, she gasps. "Oh fucking Christ. Please tell me that Hunter isn't . . . that your girls . . ."

Jackie's face turns ghostly white. She grabs each of her granddaughters by the hand and helps them out of their chairs. "Girls, let's go find out what's for dessert."

"But—" Addy says.

"Not right now, sweetheart. Come with me."

As soon as they're out of the room, Karma's lips tilt up in a feline smile. "You can be stepmother to your nieces too. Don't worry."

"What the fuck? You're saying those are my kids?" Hunter's expression is aghast as he stares at the doorway Aunt Jackie just left through. "And you never said a goddamn thing? Why?"

Karma lowers a hand to her belly, tightening the billowy fabric of the dress over her rounded stomach.

A baby bump?

"You're pregnant?" My question comes out on a shocked cry.

"I didn't want those girls to be yours," she says to Hunter, her tone suddenly devoid of laughter. "They weren't supposed to be yours. It was an accident. They were supposed to be Ricky's. *He* was supposed to get me pregnant. It just took longer for that to happen than I thought it would."

I blink twice and then once more, staring at my cousin.

"Wait. What the fuck?" I exhale on a strangled breath. "You and Ricky . . ."

Karma's expression turns deadly. "He loved me. He never loved you. And then you fucking pushed him over the edge and he wouldn't listen to reason. He just wanted the drugs. He didn't even know about the baby when he died."

Confusion swirls through my brain as I try to piece together what she's saying. "You were in LA that night?"

"I jumped on a flight as soon as he told me what you did. I tried to comfort him. But you had already ruined everything. He sent me away, and it was all your fault!"

"Screw Ricky Rango," Cricket yells. "I want to know why the hell you didn't say anything until now about Hunter! What the hell is wrong with you? You're my goddamned sister, and you were going to let me get married and never tell me any of this? How could you do this?"

"Because I didn't think you needed to know—yet. Don't worry, I was going to tell him eventually. *After* the wedding. I figured we'd find out just how much he was willing to pay to keep his little secret instead of losing you."

"You fucking bitch," Hunter says, but Lincoln clamps a hand on his shoulder as Cricket leans against my side for support. I wrap an arm around her body to keep her upright.

"This can't be happening," she whispers, her voice breaking. She jerks away from me to reach out, and the sound of her palm cracking against Karma's cheek rings out in the room. "How dare you? You are *dead to me.*"

Cricket whirls and bolts toward the door.

"Baby, wait," Hunter calls out.

My cousin pauses and turns back, shaking her head. "No. I have to go." Tears spill down her cheeks as she runs out of the room.

"Cricket!" Hunter yells, but Lincoln holds him back.

"I'll go after her," I say before heading for the door.

Cricket's already out of sight, but Jackie is standing in the alcove with the girls.

"What happened?"

"You need to talk to Karma. It's . . . it's bad."

Jackie's brows draw together and I run for the elevators, intent on getting to my cousin as quickly as possible.

LINCOLN

EVERYONE in the room stares at Karma, and I guarantee not a single thought in anyone's mind is complimentary.

"What the fuck is wrong with you?" Hunter asks her. "I don't even know what to say to you. You fucking have my kids, and then what? Pass them off as someone else's?"

"I did what I had to do. Ricky had a hell of a lot more money than you, and he did right by them. That's what matters."

"You fucking bitch."

"Hey, man, calm down. This isn't gonna help," Asa says.

My friend whips his head toward Whitney's brother. "She just ruined my goddamn wedding to the woman of my dreams . . . and you want me to fucking calm down? I need to talk to Cricket."

He pulls away from my hold, but Jackie hits the doorway with her granddaughters, and Hunter freezes as soon as he sees them.

The two little brown-haired girls stare at their mom as

Hunter locks his eyes on them. All the tension drains from his muscles as he drops into a chair and rests his elbows on the table. "Jesus Christ."

Jackie looks from him to Karma to the girls, and she's no doubt thinking what we're all thinking. *How didn't we see it before?*

And now Karma says she's pregnant . . . with Ricky Rango's kid. A kid that could possibly carry Riscoff blood in its veins, if Renee was somehow telling the truth.

Fucking hell.

"I'm going to go check on my sister and my cousin," Asa says.

"I'm going with you," Hunter and I both reply.

"Karma, what did you do?" Whitney's aunt asks quietly. "Please tell me that you didn't—"

"Don't lecture me, Mom. You don't have a whole lot of room to talk."

Jackie sucks in a harsh breath like her daughter just stabbed her, and I don't even want to know what she's talking about. All I care about right now is Whitney and her cousin and my best friend.

"Let's go," I say to Hunter as Asa disappears. We catch up to him at the elevator because he doesn't have a key card to open it.

"Havalin, you need to back the fuck off my cousin right now. I think I understand what the hell just happened, and if Karma's telling the truth, Cricket needs some space."

"I didn't know. I didn't fucking know. Karma played me. She fucking played me."

"You think I'm going to believe—"

"She did it to me too, Gable, and you fucking know it."

Asa's gaze meets mine, and I know he remembers just as well as I do the beating he gave me when Karma pretended to be Cricket and took the letter I wrote to Whitney.

He swears under his breath. "What a goddamn goat fuck."

We all step into the elevator, and I swipe my card across the key reader before hitting the button for the VIP floor. We ride up in silence, but Asa speaks when it opens.

"If Cricket doesn't want to see you, you're not forcing your way in. I don't give a damn what you have to say."

Hunter clenches his jaw so hard, I'm surprised his teeth don't crack. "You can't keep me away from her."

Asa glances at me and then back to Hunter. "I can and I will."

WHITNEY

WHEN THE KNOCK comes on the door, I already know it has to be Hunter.

"I don't want to see anyone," Cricket says on a sob. "Not Hunter, not Karma, not Mom. No one. I can't do this right now."

"Okay, honey. I promise you don't have to see anyone you don't want to see. I'll keep them all out."

Cricket sniffles into the pillows. "I just want to run away. I don't want this to be real. How could she ruin this too?"

I have absolutely no answers for my cousin, but I squeeze her hand. "I'm so sorry, Cricket."

"*She's my sister!*"

I walk to the door of the suite and open it to find my brother, Lincoln, and Hunter all waiting outside.

Hunter's Adam's apple works as he swallows. He looks absolutely destroyed and completely frantic to get to Cricket. But I also don't blame my cousin for the instructions she just gave me. Still, I feel bad for how Hunter is going to react when I break it to him.

"Cricket just wants to be left alone for a while."

"Please, Whitney. I love her so fucking much. I didn't know. All this time, I thought . . ."

"I know, and I'm sorry. She just needs some time to figure out what this means."

My brother steps forward, and I put up a hand. "She really doesn't want to see *anyone*."

"Fuck. How are we supposed to fix this then?" Asa asks, and Hunter looks like he's about to rip his hair out.

"Just give her time." I look up at Lincoln. "She wants to run away for a little while."

"She can't—" Hunter starts but cuts himself off, like he realizes he might not have any grounds to object. "Fuck. I just want to hold her and tell her I'm sorry. I didn't know. Please, just let me apologize."

"Maybe in a little while . . ."

Lincoln's gaze sharpens. I don't know what he's planning, but I know his brain is working something out.

"Come on, man. Let's get a drink at the bar and talk it through. Jackie and Karma and the girls will be coming back up, and we all have a lot to figure out."

Hunter's voice drops to a whisper. "I can't believe I have kids."

"Paternity test, man. I wouldn't trust her, even if she is my cousin." Asa chimes in, and I hate to say that I agree with him. I wouldn't trust Karma as far as I could throw her.

Lincoln nods. "Not a bad idea. You really don't know anything yet—"

"I saw their faces. They have my father's nose. And the timing is right. My gut says she's not lying."

"Come on, let's go get that drink." Lincoln guides Hunter away from the door, and I'm surprised he goes so easily. Maybe he's shell-shocked over what happened.

As soon as I close the door on them, I hurry back to Cricket. "Did you hear that?"

She lifts her tearstained face off the pillow. "I can't get married tomorrow. I can't. Not now. Not here. Not after this." More tears spill from her eyes. "I get it now."

"Get what?" I ask her.

"How you felt when you wanted to run away from everything."

I hate the brokenness in her expression and in her tone. I want to make everything right in Cricket's world, but I have no idea how to make that happen after this bomb Karma dropped. I let the rest of the horrible truth play through my mind.

My cousin was my husband's mistress, and now she says she's pregnant with his baby.

The press and his fans are going to riot again, and everyone is going to be caught in the crosshairs.

Maybe Cricket's right. Maybe running away is exactly what we need to do. And I have an idea . . .

"If I could get us out of here and somewhere no one could bother us, would you go?" I ask her.

Cricket swipes at her tears. "Yes. God, yes."

"Give me a minute."

I head back into the living room to find where I left my purse and pull out my phone. There's already a text showing on the screen.

LINCOLN: *Tell me what you need me to do. I'm here.*

I QUICKLY TYPE OUT A RESPONSE.

WHITNEY: *The chopper and Blue House. Cricket said the wedding isn't happening.*

LINCOLN: *Okay. We have to find a way to tell Hunter. I'll have the chopper on the roof within the hour.*

WHITNEY: *Thank you.*

LINCOLN: *Anything for you. I love you, Blue.*

WHITNEY: *What about Hunter?*

LINCOLN: *He's going to need to hear it from Cricket that the wedding is off.*

WHITNEY: *She doesn't want to talk to him right now.*

LINCOLN: *Then I'll handle him. I can only keep him away for so long, though.*

WHITNEY: *Just give us a few days.*

LINCOLN: *Done.*

LINCOLN

I'VE NEVER BEEN SO glad in my life that we cleared out the hotel tower for the weekend. Mrs. Havalin rails at her son in the lobby, and it looks like it's taking all of Hunter's restraint not to throttle her for the words coming out of her mouth.

I'm going to be the next one he wants to kill because I'm planning his fiancée's escape. What a damn disaster.

"Mother, if you say one more thing about the Gable family, you will regret never having a relationship with your grandchildren."

"You don't even know if those—"

"I'm going to marry Cricket come hell or high water, and we're going to have a houseful of kids. Whether what Karma says is true or not, you're risking a hell of a lot if you keep going." Hunter's tone leaves absolutely no room for argument, but Mrs. Havalin just can't take the hint.

"I can't believe you still want to marry that girl—"

"Woman, enough. We're going home." Mr. Havalin finally speaks again, and then looks at his son. "What do you want us to do? Do you want us to tell everyone the wedding is off?"

"I need to talk to Cricket first," Hunter replies.

I take that as my cue. "Cricket told Whitney there won't be a wedding tomorrow. She'd like a few days to sort everything out. I'm really sorry, man. So fucking sorry."

"Fuck!" Hunter turns, no doubt looking for a wall to punch.

Surprisingly, Asa joins us and helps me try to talk Hunter down. "Give her a few days, man. Cricket can't hold a grudge. She's got too soft of a heart. She's not going to let this stop you guys from having a future."

"I just want to fucking talk to her!" Hunter roars, and I empathize.

I've been there. After the accident, all I wanted was to get to Whitney, and no one would let me. I glance at Asa, and his expression tells me he's not going to let Hunter see Cricket unless she agrees. Fucker.

"If she loved you enough to agree to marry you, she's not going to shut you out for long," Asa says.

My best friend is going to hit the roof when he realizes he won't have a choice. I have to tell him now.

"They're going to Blue House."

"What?" Hunter asks as he turns to face me.

"The chopper is coming. I told her I wouldn't be able to keep you away for long."

"You motherfucking—" Hunter lunges at me, and shockingly, Asa steps in the way.

"Let her go, Havalin. Get the paternity test done. Then you'll know where you stand. Right?"

My friend spins around and jams his hands into his hair. "Fucking hell!"

WHITNEY

THE CHOPPER TOUCHES down on the landing pad, and its lights shine out on the ocean waves crashing in the darkness beyond the sea wall. This is as far as I got last time, before Lincoln and I were called back to Gable. I'm almost afraid to set foot on the ground because of what could possibly happen this time, but for Cricket's sake, I say nothing as we climb out. Thankfully, the torrential rain stopped halfway into our flight, and now a woman stands on the edge of the helipad and waves us over.

"Hi!" she says over the beating rotors. "I'm Janelle. My husband and I are the caretakers here. Welcome to Blue House."

"Thank you so much," I yell.

"We'll get your bags. Please feel free to head inside. We have light refreshments waiting for you. I'll show you around as soon as you've had a chance to relax."

Cricket follows beside me, a stunned expression on her face as we walk toward the gorgeous house. It's blue, as its name would suggest, but a dark grayish tone that no doubt matches the color of the ocean on stormy days.

"Wow. This is . . . incredible," she says as Janelle shows us to a living area with a massive picture window that must have the most incredible view of the sea during the day. A white sectional sofa forms a *U* shape around a table with chilled white wine, fruit, and a charcuterie board.

"Let me know if there's anything else at all I can get you. I'm a chef, so there's pretty much nothing I can't make, even when we're low on provisions."

"Cricket? Is there anything specific you want?"

My cousin shakes her head, continuing to stare out the window. "This is great. Thank you so much."

"You can find me in the kitchen." Janelle points toward a doorway across the room. "Which is through there, whenever you're ready for your tour. I'll have your bags stowed in your rooms right now."

"Thank you," I tell her again, and she disappears through the doorway she indicated moments ago.

When we're alone, I touch Cricket's arm. "Do you want food?"

I gesture to the table, falling into the hostess role easily, which should be strange, but it's not. Even though I've never been in this house, I feel totally at ease.

Lincoln was right. This place is special.

Cricket shakes her head. "I'm not hungry. But the wine, on the other hand . . ."

Do I think my cousin getting trashed right now is the best idea ever? No, not really, but then again, she did just find out her fiancé has two kids with her sister, *who tricked him into sleeping with her.*

"All the wine for both of us," I say.

We make ourselves comfortable on the couch and reach for the glasses of white. The crisp, tart flavor is refreshing after the flight, and Cricket drains hers quickly and reaches for the bottle for a refill.

It's on the tip of my tongue to tell her to slow down, but that's not what we're here for. We're here so she can escape, and however she needs to do that is her choice. I wouldn't be surprised if she broke out her own stash and rolled a joint right here.

I pick at the food because it seems like a shame to let it go to waste, and wait for her to speak.

"I guess if I had to run away from my own wedding, we could've picked a worse place."

"I'm so sorry, Cricket." I kick off my sandals and curl my feet beneath me on the large sectional sofa. I lean into her and wrap an arm around her shoulders.

She shakes her head. "Don't be sorry. You didn't do it. My sister fucked me. Or should I say, fucked me *and Hunter*."

I swallow the bile that rises in my throat at the thought. If Karma had done that to me, I'd have been hard-pressed not to shred her face with my claws. Latent jealous instincts push to the forefront when I think of her potentially putting her hands on Lincoln.

"Actually, I should say she fucked *both our men*."

Cricket's comment takes me aback, because I'd already forgotten to care that Karma had been cheating with Ricky —while we were married. I can't actually muster up a single drop of jealousy to waste on that.

Huh. So that's the difference when you find the right man. You're willing to go to war to keep the one you love.

If I needed any further proof that what I have with Lincoln is completely and totally different, that would be another piece.

But tonight isn't about me. It's about Cricket.

"I know, but I still hate it most for you. Tonight and tomorrow were supposed to be everything you've ever wanted, and she ruined it."

Cricket shrugs, and I release her. "If you want to know the truth . . . it all felt wrong." She glances away, but I catch the guilty look on her face.

"What do you mean?"

"The Gables, the fancy setup, all those people Mrs. Havalin invited that I didn't know. I didn't want that. I just wanted Hunter and me and something simple." She pauses to take another sip. "Maybe Karma did me a favor. This wasn't going to be the wedding of my dreams. It was turning into a nightmare. You heard how she was at the rehearsal. It was awful. It took everything I had not to run out and call it off then."

Guilt that I didn't stand up sooner to Mrs. Havalin swirls in my belly. But part of me wonders if there's something more important that Cricket isn't saying.

"Do you still want to get married?" I ask, and her forlorn expression crushes me. "Oh, Cricket." I wrap both arms around her as tears tip over her lids.

"I just let it get too far. I absolutely want to marry Hunter, if he still wants me after tonight. But not like that. It wasn't me. But I didn't want to give Mrs. Havalin any more reason to disapprove of me, so I just let her do what she wanted. I didn't want to rock the boat." She hiccups as she finishes.

"I'm so sorry, babe. I did a terrible job standing up for

you and making sure you weren't getting steamrolled. That's why you wanted me here, and I failed you."

Cricket shakes her head. "No, because I shouldn't have needed someone to speak up for me. I should've been able to do it myself. But I was so afraid that Hunter would be disappointed in me. That he'd realize I wasn't the person he was supposed to be with, because I was too different from what his mother wanted for him."

"Oh, honey. Don't say that." Even as I console Cricket, I can relate to her feelings perfectly. If Mrs. Riscoff were still alive, her presence would definitely impact my relationship with Lincoln.

"All those reasons you're giving are exactly why he loves you. And if Hunter were dumb enough to ever to listen to his mother over your express wishes, he wouldn't deserve you."

My cousin looks down at her clasped hands. "I know. But I still can't shut down that voice in my head telling me it'd be easier if we weren't together."

"But would it make you happier if you weren't together?"

Her face lifts to mine, and sadness is etched into her features. "No. I already hate myself for running away from him, but there was no way I could stay and face everything for another minute without breaking."

Cricket bursts into tears again, and I hold her tight, letting her cry out all of her confusion and despair.

"We're going to figure it out. I promise."

"But if Karma's telling the truth . . ."

"Shhh," I tell her as she hiccups again. "Let's just worry about one thing at a time. You love Hunter, and he loves you. You can figure out everything else later."

After we finish our wine and Cricket passes out on the couch, I find a blanket and use it to cover her. I tuck myself in at the other end and pull out my phone.

WHITNEY: Bring Hunter tomorrow. Cricket needs him.

LINCOLN: I wouldn't be able to keep him away even if I tried. Love you and miss you already.

LINCOLN

I'VE NEVER SEEN Hunter so calm and controlled as I did last night when he spoke to Karma, and she basically told him that if Ricky Rango hadn't died, she never would have told Hunter the twins were his. She was too busy collecting her payment for "child support" every month from the idiot rock star because she'd been sleeping with him on and off for ten years.

It took every ounce of self-control I possessed not to pick her up and shake her for that. How is it possible for one woman to cause so much destruction?

And then there was Hunter's mother. Mrs. Havalin had to be removed from the premises at The Gables under threats of being sedated after Mr. Havalin rushed her out of the room where the rehearsal dinner was being held. She left the hotel ranting that no one was allowed to jilt her son, and the entire Havalin family would be humiliated by the fact that the wedding was canceled.

No one gave a single damn what she thought, especially her son.

The only thing Hunter cares about is Cricket, and that has never been clearer as we approach Blue House in the chopper.

My best friend sits across from me, his hands clenched into fists. Waves of stress roll off him, and I can't say I blame the man. He knows he's got the fight of his life on his hands.

"I love her," Hunter says, his voice hoarse. "I fucking love Cricket more than I thought I could ever love someone in my life, and I fucked it up by sleeping with her sister—when I thought I was with her." He glances toward the window. "How can she ever forgive me for that?"

"There's nothing to forgive. You didn't know. She loves you too, man. You both just need time to process this and figure out how to move forward."

"I have two fucking kids, and I didn't know it!"

"And Cricket loves those little girls like crazy already because they're her nieces."

Hunter drops his head into his hands, his elbows braced on his knees. "And so did I, because they were *her nieces*. But they're mine. Jesus, fuck. I can't believe I have two daughters. Twin girls. And with Karma fucking Gable. You know she's going to use them to fuck with me and Cricket, if Cricket will even see me again. Karma won't hesitate to manipulate both of us by using them."

I know my friend is dead-on. Karma Gable is a narcissistic opportunist. Nothing is ever her fault. Everyone owes her something. She'll never hesitate to use an opening, even her own children, for her own gain. That has already been proven by the way she played Rango.

"How did I not know she wasn't Cricket? I should've known."

"She's a great actress, man. Trust me, I can tell you all about it. She fooled me too. I was trying to get a letter to Whitney the day of her parents' funeral. I thought I was giving it to Cricket, but it was Karma. She deliberately misled me. This isn't a new game for her. You didn't have a chance."

"I should've known something was wrong. When I tried to talk to Cricket after that and she seemed confused, how could I not have picked up on it? I thought she was playing hard to get. And then when I finally manned up to try again a few years later, it should've occurred to me that Cricket would never have played those kinds of games. How could I have been so fucking stupid?"

Hunter turns toward the window, but I catch the look of anguish on his face. He's tearing himself apart over this, and there's nothing I'll be able to say to make him stop. Cricket is the only one who can do that.

"Look, what happened in the past is over and done with. Now it's time to move forward. You have two kids who need a dad, regardless of what Karma might say, and you and Cricket are going to be fine. You just have to give her a little time."

Over our headsets, the pilot announces our position to the tower. I know we're almost to Blue House, where Whitney's aware of our impending arrival, but Cricket isn't. Which was Whitney's idea.

I just hope she's right about this. I don't want to see my friend shredded any more than he already has been. They were both victims of Karma's scheming, and Whitney too.

When the chopper approaches the helipad, I can see

two women sitting by the pool in bikinis. One jumps up, wrapping a towel around herself. Hunter sees her too.

We're barely on the ground when Hunter throws open the door and vaults out of the helicopter, heading in a dead sprint toward Cricket's shocked form.

As I climb out, I hope like hell she isn't going to run from him.

She doesn't.

Cricket drops the towel and throws herself into Hunter's arms, and I send up a little prayer of thanks to anyone who might be listening. As I walk over to them, Whitney rises and wraps a towel around her waist. She meets me on the path to the helipad.

"You made it here a lot quicker than I expected."

"We left early. Someone was in a hurry. How is Cricket?"

"She's confused. Upset. Betrayed. But mostly she's pissed at Karma and brokenhearted for Maddy and Addy that their mom has been using them to get money for all these years."

I pull her into my arms. "And you? How do you feel?"

Whitney's expression turns reflective. "I'm surprisingly a lot less upset than you would expect. I already knew Ricky was cheating. The fact that he was cheating with my own cousin . . . it's a slap in the face, but I wouldn't put anything past Karma anymore. If I loved him, it would've been a lot harder to swallow, but I'm actually pretty numb about the whole thing."

I press a kiss to her forehead. "I'm glad you're not going to let it bring you down."

"No, but I do feel bad for the girls. They shouldn't be

used like pawns, and to find out about their dad that way
. . ."

"Brutal," I add in agreement when she trails off.

"Yeah. Not fair at all."

Ahead of us, Cricket climbs Hunter like a tree and is kissing him frantically. So frantically, it's actually awkward to watch, but it's better than the alternative.

When he lowers her to the ground, she grabs his hand and drags him toward the house. Whitney and I watch as they disappear inside.

She presses her lips together, but the corners curve upward. "That went about as well as can be expected."

I laugh, because there's nothing else to do in this situation. "Definitely."

I glance down at her bikini-clad body appreciatively. With everything that has happened recently, we haven't had a chance to just *be*, and if Cricket and Hunter are going to hide away in the house, then I'm going to take every opportunity I have to spend time alone with Whitney.

"You want to change into your suit?" she asks.

While there are a lot of things I want to do with her, including get her *out* of her suit, right now, seeing the sunshine glint off her black hair is at the top of my list.

"I've got clothes inside. Did Janelle show you to the master bedroom?"

"This morning. We sort of passed out on the couch last night after Cricket drank a few glasses of wine."

I grasp Whitney's hand, and together we walk toward the house.

"Why did you call this Blue House?" she asks, her voice carrying a hint of shyness.

I look down into her gorgeous blue eyes. "Why do you think, Blue?"

Her shy smile widens. "Because you like the color?"

"Because I love *you.*"

I pull her into my chest as she wraps her arms around my neck.

"So much that you named a house after me?"

"It was my refuge. Just like you were," I say, then correct myself. "Just like you *are.*"

"I love it, by the way. But not as much as I love you."

WHITNEY

IT TAKES us a couple of hours to re-emerge from Lincoln's bedroom, and when we do, both of us are smiling. The noise from Cricket's room finally quieted, but it's safe to say that she and Hunter have made up, and will find a way to work this out.

Janelle sets out lunch on the terrace by the pool, and Lincoln and I settle into the chairs. The view from every single place I've stood on this island and in the house is absolutely incredible. It's truly a place that I could see us coming to for years. Our own safe haven away from the world where we can forget everything and just enjoy each other.

Ten years ago, we only had stolen hours here and there, and I think that's what made that time seem even more precious—because we both knew it was fleeting.

Now I want all the time in the world with this man, but I know when we're in Gable, there will always be other things competing for his attention. But not here. At Blue House, Lincoln can be mine alone.

"What are you thinking about?" he asks as he takes a sip of ice water.

"That I hope this can be our place, where the world doesn't get to intrude. Like the cabin was all those years ago."

Something glints in Lincoln's eyes, and I can't help but wonder what he's thinking.

"I'm glad you feel that way. Blue House has always been special, but mostly because I always wanted to show it to you. I wanted to know what you would think of this place." His attention drops to the table, and he pauses.

"What?"

He looks up, his hazel gaze shimmering with sincerity. "I built Blue House for you. For us." He laughs, shaking his head. "I thought I was fucking crazy at the time. Who would build a house on an island for a woman married to another man?"

His admission rocks me.

"Are you serious?"

Lincoln nods. "I knew we weren't done. I refused to accept it. If it took me until my last breath, I was going to get my second chance with you."

Tears sting my eyes, but they have nothing to do with sadness. No, these are happy tears.

"Really?"

He nods again. "I don't give up easily, and for you, I was never giving up." Lincoln rises from his seat and steps around the table. "I wasn't planning to do this now, but I wasn't *not* planning to do it now either . . ."

"What?" I blink as he drops to one knee and pulls something out of his pocket and holds it up between us.

"You're the only woman I've ever seen when I

154

pictured forever, and now I know forever with you still isn't long enough, but it'll have to do. Whitney Gable, will you marry me?"

My mouth drops open as a sense of disbelief takes over my system. The tears that were burning my eyes only moments ago materialize and spill down my cheeks as the sun catches the diamond and it flashes.

I cover my mouth with both hands as I stumble from my chair and drop to my knees before him. He pulls one hand away from my mouth and holds the ring at the end of my finger.

"Will you?"

"Of course! Of course I'll marry you!"

I'm laughing and crying, and my hand shakes as he slides the diamond onto it. But it has nothing to do with fear or uncertainty, and everything to do with the fact that it's official.

I've never been this happy in my entire life.

Lincoln Riscoff is finally mine, and I'm his.

LINCOLN

"Oh shit, we're interrupting."

Cricket's voice comes from behind me moments after I pull Whitney to her feet and kiss the hell out of my future wife.

I tear my lips away for a moment. "Go away. Come back later."

"Shut up!" She must see the rock on Whitney's hand because she squeals and comes racing toward us. "You're engaged? Oh my God! This is, like, the second-best news of the day!"

Whitney wipes away the tears streaking down her cheeks to look at her cousin. "And what's the best news of the day?"

"We're getting married!" Cricket grabs Hunter's hand. "But not today. When we want to. How we want to. Where we want to."

"And my mother can either accept it or not come," Hunter adds.

The smile on Whitney's face widens even further as she springs toward her cousin to hug her.

"I'm so glad! This is the best day." She turns around to look at me. "I think Blue House might be magic."

I don't have to tell her I already knew that.

CRICKET AND HUNTER join us for lunch, and being surrounded by such joy is a completely new experience for me. Janelle brings us champagne, and we toast each other until we're buzzed.

Nothing can touch us here. No one can take this away from us.

We eat until we can't eat any more, and Whitney and I sink into one of the plush cushions on a large round chair by the pool. Cricket and Hunter laze across from us, side by side and holding hands. We probably all look like the most disgusting pictures of happiness.

Fucking finally.

"We need some music," Cricket says, pulling out her phone. She taps the screen a couple of times, and the first sound to come out of it has Whitney curling away from me.

It takes me a few seconds to realize that the voice is Ricky Rango's. *But the words are Whitney's.*

"Shit. Sorry."

"No, don't change it," I say.

Whitney looks at me funny. "Why not? We don't need him here. He'll just ruin everything."

I shake my head. "No, he won't. Because he doesn't have that power anymore. Besides, he didn't write those

157

words. You did. It might be his voice, but this is your heart."

"I never thought about it like that," Whitney whispers. It takes a moment before she relaxes into me, but when she does, her spine unbends and she starts to hum along with it.

"I wrote this song thinking about you," she says when it ends, and the words I just heard hit home even harder.

"I'm so sorry I put you in the position where he had even a sliver of a chance with you. I hate that I gave Renee the opening she needed to threaten you. I'm so sorry, Whitney. You'll never know how sorry."

She shakes her head. "Don't be sorry. It might not have been the road I wanted to travel, but it led me right back here to you. This is where I was meant to be, and I appreciate every single bit of it more now than I ever could have before. This is *real*. This is *perfect*."

"This is us," I tell her quietly.

The song changes to something else, and we spend the afternoon exactly the way it was meant to be spent.

Together.

WHITNEY

BY THE TIME dinner rolls around, Cricket has the mad urge to have a bonfire on the beach, and Lincoln indulges her.

Once the flames crackle in the firepit, we roast hot dogs and I laugh as Lincoln tries to figure out how to get his off the stick and into the bun.

"You've never done this before, have you?"

He shakes his head. "No, but clearly I've been missing out."

As we eat half-charred dogs with too much ketchup, I sip wine out of a plastic tumbler and stare up at the stars.

Cricket and Hunter sit across the fire from us, and it makes me so happy to see them just like they were before Karma dropped her bomb on all of us. *She can't break them.* Just like nothing can break Lincoln and me. I truly believe that now. Our relationship has been forged in the fires of adversity, and we've emerged as something different. Something beautiful in a way that we never could have been before.

I try to think about what it would have been like if I

hadn't married Ricky, and Lincoln and I had stayed together after that summer. Whatever would have followed could never have been as strong and precious, because we now know what it's like to lose the person you love most.

"Whit, why don't you sing us one of your songs? I know you've been writing like a fiend."

I lift my gaze to stare across the fire at my cousin. She knows I don't sing. My voice is strictly for shower-only performances.

"How do you know that?" I ask, deflecting the question.

"Because I heard you last night after you texted Lincoln and you thought I was asleep."

I narrow my gaze on my cousin. "You sly bitch."

Her smile, complete with ketchup at the corner of her mouth, melts my heart. "Come on. You haven't sung for me in years. You used to kill me with how amazing you were."

I stare at Cricket like she's taken a bad trip. "I think your memory is broken, because whoever you're remembering wasn't me."

She shakes her head. "No, definitely you. Because I remember you singing that first single before it ever hit the radio. Acoustic. In the backyard. We were both buzzed off crappy wine coolers and dreaming about the future."

As soon as she describes that night, the memory blooms in my brain like I can see it playing out in real time.

She's right. I did sing for her.

"I'm not drunk enough to do that again."

"I want to hear you." Lincoln's voice comes out husky,

and his breath skims across my ear. "I would love to hear you, actually."

I shake my head, apprehension creeping into my veins. "No. You really don't. I'm not good. The songs might be good—I can admit that—but I'm not. I'm a songwriter, not a singer."

"She's full of shit, for the record," Cricket says, and I want to slap her.

"Leave her alone, babe. If she doesn't want to sing, don't push her." Hunter comes to my rescue but also grabs the bottle of wine by the neck. "But if you need a little liquid courage, I can get you a refill."

Lincoln plucks the tumbler out of my hand and leans around the fire, his long body curving until Hunter can refill my cup.

When it's back in my hand, I take a long, deep drink. Just the thought of anyone hearing me sing now threatens to break me out in hives. Ricky used to laugh at my voice, and told me not to let anyone hear me because it would be too embarrassing for him, and for me.

Asshole.

I shove the thought out of my head, because I refuse to let memories like that pollute this incredible place and this amazing time.

"Sorry, Whit. I didn't mean to make you uncomfortable. You know that's the last thing I'd ever want to do. I just . . . I remember how incredible you were, and then one day you just . . . stopped, and I never heard you again."

"Because someone told me the truth about how I really sounded."

Cricket sits up in Hunter's arms, sloshing wine over the rim of her tumbler. "Wait a minute. Are you telling me that piece of shit convinced you that you were *bad*? If he weren't dead, I'd kill him right now." Hunter has to wrap an arm around Cricket to keep her from charging toward me.

"Babe, give her some space."

Behind me, Lincoln stiffens, and I want to end this whole conversation as quickly as it started. And there's one really good way to do that—humiliate myself in front of all of them. At least it'll ensure that they never ask again.

I gulp down half my wine and rise to my feet.

"Blue—"

I turn away from the fire, facing the swift winds rising off the ocean, and wave a hand behind me to stop Lincoln from doing whatever he's about to do.

I close my eyes and start quietly, sending my voice into the darkness with the heat of the fire and their gazes on my back.

"I never wanted to be stronger.

I just wanted to be yours.

To steal a little longer . . ."

Gaining a little more courage as my voice seemed to be carried away by the breeze, I keep going, diving into the first verse of the song I've been working on for days.

I raise my tumbler as I hit the chorus again. And then the bridge.

By the time I finish, I'm convinced that no one heard me, and only the waves experienced the voice I've learned to keep hidden. But when I turn around, I know I'm wrong.

Cricket's smile threatens to break her face, and tears

shine in her eyes. Hunter starts a slow clap, and suddenly, I'm terrified to look at Lincoln.

"Blue . . . why didn't you tell me?"

His voice is a beacon for my gaze. He's already standing, his body tense. And his face . . . there's something so pure shining on it, I'm afraid to believe it's real.

Pride.

"You sound . . . you're incredible," he says.

Cricket claps louder than Hunter. "She's a goddamn angel who's been silenced for too long."

Lincoln walks toward me, dodging the fire. When he stops in front of me, his palms curve around my cheeks.

"You were amazing before, but you need to know that whatever you've thought all these years about your voice —it was wrong. I don't have to love you to know how special your talent is."

Tears trickle down my cheeks, and Lincoln wipes them away with his thumbs.

"You think so?"

"I know so."

LINCOLN

I COULD KILL Rango for what he did to Whitney. *Fucking kill him.*

Feeling her body vibrate with fear gutted me and made me wish I could take back my request. Watching her rise, her posture stiff and uncomfortable, made me want to snatch her back into my arms where I could keep her safe.

But listening to her belt out heart-breaking lyrics into the wind in a voice that was pure and sweet unleashed a wave of pride in me that may never be duplicated. Not just because of her talent, but because of the risk she took to conquer that fear.

Whitney Gable is truly the most extraordinary woman I've ever had the pleasure to know. I'm the luckiest man in the whole goddamned world that she's wearing my ring and is going to spend the rest of her life with me.

I knew she was special the day she walked into that bar, but I didn't know she was the one until I lost her. I paid for that for ten years, and then I almost fucked it up again.

"I will never deserve you," I tell her as I wipe the tears away from her face. "But I'll never stop trying."

Her tears fall faster as my lips take hers, and in the moonlight, beneath the stars, I seal that vow with a kiss. When I pull away, Whitney's tears slow.

"I love you, Lincoln."

"I love you more, so goddamn much." I wrap my arms around her waist and pick her up, carrying her away from the fire and back toward the house.

From behind us, I hear Cricket laugh.

"So, what does everyone think about a double wedding?"

I'm too busy carrying Whitney in my arms and taking her to bed to answer.

WHITNEY

THE LAST TIME my phone rang on this island with a call from Jackie, all hell broke loose. When I stare down at it on the breakfast bar and see her name on the display, the last thing I want to do is answer it and shatter the peace we've finally found.

The island and Blue House have healed us all in a way that I couldn't have predicted. The sparkle of the ring on my finger tells me that I didn't make it up. All of this is real.

The phone vibrates again, and I know I have no choice but to answer.

"Hey, Jackie, everything okay back at the ranch?" I inject as much lightness into my tone as possible, as if I'm hoping that will influence the direction of the call.

"You need to come back. Both you and Cricket." My aunt, who is normally rock solid and calm, even in the face of disaster, bursts into a sob.

I look over to where Cricket and Hunter sit by the pool, his arms wrapped loosely around her as the wind blows her brown hair. Goose bumps rise on my arms.

I knew I didn't want to answer this call.

"What's going on?" I try to keep my tone calm, but even I can hear the panic creeping in.

"Karma . . . she's in the hospital."

Oh Jesus. What now? "Is it the baby?"

"There's no baby, Whit. She . . . she thought she was pregnant, but . . ."

My brows dive together in confusion. "What are you talking about? I saw the bump. She said—"

"She has ovarian cancer. The bump was a tumor. They have to operate—"

When Jackie cuts off mid-sentence with another sob, guilt immediately crushes me for all the awful thoughts I've been having about Karma. My elbow lands on the breakfast bar hard enough to rattle the dishes.

Lincoln's head jerks at the sound, and he must see the horrified expression on my face. He rushes toward me, ready to do battle with whoever might be on the other end of the phone call for upsetting me.

I reach out, and he grasps my hand. "We'll be there as soon as we can, Jackie. I'm so, so sorry. I love you."

She dissolves into sobs and whispers out a quiet *thank you* before the call ends.

"What?" Lincoln asks.

"Get the chopper. We have to go to the hospital, and I have no idea how the hell I'm going to tell Cricket."

LINCOLN and I climb out of the chopper after it lands on

the helipad in front of the Riscoff Memorial Hospital, but Cricket sits frozen inside.

Hunter unhooks her buckles and guides her to the door, but she looks like a zombie. As soon as they clear the blades, I thread my fingers through hers and squeeze her hand.

"Are you—" I start to ask if she's okay, but Cricket speaks before I can get the question out.

"I was so mad at her. She ruined everything. I wanted her to hurt like she made everyone else hurt. I said I wanted her dead, *and now she has cancer.*" Cricket's stricken expression breaks my heart. "What kind of horrible person am I? She—"

"Stop. You can't think like that. It's not your fault. It didn't happen because of what she did or what you thought. It's . . . it's just life handing us another shock we didn't expect. We'll get through it, just like we've gotten through everything else. She'll have top-of-the-line care, and she'll be fine."

"The doctors here are all handpicked, and if she needs specialists, we'll fly them in right away." Lincoln's calm and reassuring tone makes me love him even more. He leans down to kiss the top of my head as he squeezes me tighter against his side.

As we walk into the hospital as a unit, I know this won't be the last time, but I wish it were. Especially because it seems like our lives are irrevocably changed every time we step through these doors.

It terrifies me what changes could possibly come now, but like I told Cricket—we'll get through it. We don't have any other option.

Jackie meets us in the lobby, and her lined features

look like she's aged ten years since I last saw her. "Thank God, you're here." She rushes to Cricket and hugs her.

"What happened?" Cricket asks with tears already running down her cheeks. "Where are the girls?"

"Ms. Gable has a nanny with them at the hotel for now. Karma didn't want them to see her like this."

Hunter's expression creases, and I wonder if he's thinking that if Karma isn't lying, it's his responsibility to take care of the girls because she can't. My heart thuds somewhere down in my stomach as the reality of the situation hits me.

It must be bad.

"What did they say?" I ask. "You mentioned surgery? When?"

"Later this afternoon. They're going to try to remove the tumor. They just did images of it. They said it's the size of a cantaloupe." Jackie bursts into tears, and Cricket squeezes her mom tight.

"Oh my God, Mom. How is this even possible? How could she think . . ."

"The doctor explained it all. Ovarian cancer mimics plenty of signs that can make you think you're actually pregnant, even a positive pregnancy test. Karma said when she took hers a month or so ago, it was positive. She never had a reason to think it was anything but another baby. She didn't go to the doctor yet because she didn't want us to find out."

I know what we're all thinking, but no one will say it, because it would make us all heartless, awful people. But the very nature of my cousin's name suggests that what goes around comes around.

I don't want her to suffer or be sick, but this seems like

life's awful way of serving her a reminder that things don't always go the way we plan.

"Can I see her?" Cricket asks.

Jackie swallows and looks sheepish. "She . . . After I called Whit, I told her you were coming, and she said she doesn't want to see any of you. She doesn't want anyone's pity. I'm so sorry. I—"

Cricket turns away, but not before I see how crushed she is by Jackie's words.

Hunter pulls her into his chest and holds her. "I'm so sorry, babe."

"Is there anything else you need or that we can do to help, Ms. Gable?" Lincoln asks.

My aunt shakes her head. "No. Everyone's been very kind. They said they're doing everything they can, and for now . . . all we can do is wait until they take her into the OR and get this awful thing out of her."

"Good. I'm glad they have a solid plan in place." Lincoln looks toward the private waiting rooms we've both sat in while life as we knew it shifted off its axis. He notices my gaze following his. "There's another waiting room up on the fourth floor, I believe. In the cancer wing. It's new and comfortable."

How is it possible that my heart feels like it's breaking for Jackie and Cricket about Karma, but is being held together by Lincoln?

"If she changes her mind about seeing anyone, I promise I'll come get you," Jackie says.

LINCOLN

I HATE FEELING powerless and helpless. I can't fix this for Whitney and her family, and with each tick of the clock in the waiting room, it's maddening. Everyone in this room has to be struggling with the same conflicting emotions. Angry at Karma for what she's done, but devastated by what she's facing. Whitney's brother ducked in to say hi, but he's taken it upon himself to stand vigil by Karma's door, whether she wants him there or not.

Jackie continues to give us updates, but it's not until the time is closing in on Karma's surgery that she asks to see someone.

Not Cricket, though.

Hunter.

"She wants to say something to you, just in case she doesn't make it out of surgery," Jackie says with a sob. She's a strong woman, but I think it's safe to say that life found her breaking point today.

"Yes, ma'am. I can do that."

He rises from his chair with a squeeze of Cricket's

hand and follows Jackie out of the room. Whitney pops out of her seat and paces while we wait.

We don't have to wait long. Hunter returns less than ten minutes later, his face grim.

"What did she say?" Cricket asks.

"She wrote a will."

"Oh Jesus," Whitney whispers.

Hunter faces Cricket, but we all listen to what he says next. "If anything happens to her, she made me promise that you and I would raise the girls and your mom could see them anytime she wanted, but that I wouldn't let them around my mom until she . . ."

"Until she what?" Cricket asks.

"Until she learns how not to be a total bitch because the girls shouldn't have to deal with that."

"Oh my God." Tears trickle even faster down Cricket's face.

Whitney pauses in the middle of the room, her teeth biting into her bottom lip. I go to her, pull her against me, and hold her.

We all stand in the room for several long minutes of silence, until I finally hear the sound of footsteps and voices in the hallway.

It's time.

Whitney turns toward the door, and together we watch as Karma is rolled down the hall in her hospital bed.

"Stop!" Cricket breaks free from Hunter's hold and rushes to the door.

Karma's face, paler than I've ever seen it before, tilts toward her sister's voice.

"I have something to say to you."

Jackie grabs Cricket's arm as she hits the threshold. "Baby, not now. She doesn't want—"

"I don't care what Karma wants right now, because if there's even a single chance this is the last time I get to talk to my sister, I'm not going to let her take it from me."

"What do you want?" Karma asks. "To scream at me and curse me for ruining your life? I think I picked up the cursed part just fine."

"No," Cricket says quietly. "I wanted to tell you that I love you and I forgive you, and no matter what happens, you'll always be my sister."

Karma's face twists, and tears shimmer in her eyes. She reaches up with her right hand and dashes them away. "If I don't . . . If this . . ." She starts to speak, but when she can't finish a thought, Cricket speaks up.

"I love Maddy and Addy more than life itself. I didn't care who their dad was before, and I don't care now. They're my nieces, no matter what." She reaches out and touches Karma's arm. "Just like you'll always be my sister, no matter what. I love you all so much."

Karma wipes away another tear and gives Cricket a nod. "I'll see you on the other side."

───

TWO HOURS INTO THE SURGERY, Asa finally talks Jackie into going to the cafeteria for something to eat before the woman tips over from exhaustion. Whitney is asleep on my shoulder when I get a call from my sister.

"I know you're busy right now, but we have a problem. A big problem."

"The media?"

"No. Worse. There's a wildfire. It's moving fast, even with the rain we had a few days ago. Everything's so dry from the entire summer that it's going up like kindling."

Fuck.

Fire is one word you never want to hear when you live in the forest on a mountain, and not only because we're in the timber business. They're not a rare occurrence, given the drought conditions that have plagued the area for years, and the higher frequency is just one more reason I've pushed to diversify the company even more.

"Where is it heading? Do they know how many acres?"

"It's coming down the mountain, and they're already calling for evacuations of homes and businesses in the impacted area. We're right in its path, Lincoln."

Fuck. "The hotel?"

"Your house, the estate, the hotel. They're all next on the list for evacuation if it gets any worse."

Whitney wakes up as I shift, and her bleary eyes focus on me as my voice roughens.

"We can rebuild, just get everyone out as soon as they make the call. Even before, if you feel like it's the right move." Another thought occurs to me. "What about Commodore's cabin?"

"Commodore's at the estate. I told him about the warning—"

"But what about Magnus Gable? Is he out of his house? Did they get him somewhere safe?"

My sister goes quiet, and Whitney's gaze locks on my face.

"What's going on?" she asks, but my sister replies.

"I don't know . . . no one said anything about him."

174

"We have to get him out. Now. If we're next on the list to evacuate, he already should have."

"The road up the mountain is closed. They've locked it down. No one can get up there."

"Then it's lucky I have a chopper out front. I'll call you when I land at the estate and get Commodore somewhere safe. If you need any help with the hotel—"

All the color drains from Whitney's face as she realizes what we're talking about.

"We've got it covered," McKinley says. "This is what we train for."

"Stay safe, Mac."

"You too, big brother."

The fact that McKinley doesn't tell me not to call her that, like she always does, drives home just how serious this threat is.

As soon as I hang up the phone, Whitney's questions come rapid-fire.

"What the hell is going on? There's a fire? Magnus might be stuck up the mountain?"

"Oh my God," Cricket says from across the room, as the image on the TV changes to show nothing but flames. The headline at the bottom reads:

MOUNTAIN TOWN OF GABLE THREATENED BY BLAZE

WHITNEY TURNS toward it and then slowly looks back at me. "I'm going with you."

WHITNEY

AUNT JACKIE, Cricket, and Hunter promised they would send updates as soon as they heard anything, but my brain puts that aside as we fly toward the inferno that used to be a forest-covered mountain.

Lincoln and I are both quiet, but his hand grips mine tighter as we fly into hell. I know he's thinking the same thing I am—this is bad. *Really fucking bad.*

Magnus and Commodore's houses are still a few miles ahead, and right on the border of the forest the fast-moving fire has already devoured.

"We have to get him out!" I yell it into my headset and Lincoln nods.

"We will. Don't worry."

My heart lodges in my throat as I see the outlines of the two cabins on the edge of the cliff. Thankfully, they're not yet engulfed in flames, but thick smoke and flying ash make it almost impossible to see the wooden siding. *Siding that will go up faster than newspaper.*

As soon as the chopper touches down, I rip off my

harness and climb out. My feet hit the ground and I take off in a dead run, yelling my great-uncle's name.

"Magnus!"

"Whitney!" Lincoln runs after me, but I don't stop.

When I reach the door, the familiar sight of a long barrel greets me as it pokes through the window, where he's cut a hole in the screen.

"I'll shoot you! Looters are only getting bullets here!"

"It's me, Whitney! We have to get you out of here, Magnus!"

Magnus lowers the rifle, and a moment later, the door opens. "What the hell are you doing here, girl? Didn't you see there's a fire coming in quick?"

"What the hell are you still doing here?" I ask him.

"Just about to make my way down to the river to float out."

Of course. Leave it to Magnus to have an escape route planned.

"We've got a helicopter. It'll be quicker."

"You don't say?" He looks out the window, and the *whap-whap* of the rotors is drowned out by the crack of trees falling in the woods and the thundering wind.

"Let's go!"

I grab the bag off the floor that I assume Magnus wants to bring. As I turn, Lincoln's there, taking it from my hand.

"Anything else, sir? Because we have to go. *Now.*"

"Then move your ass, boy. I don't want to be burned to a crisp."

With that, we all hurry to the helicopter and climb in. As soon as we're buckled in, the bird lifts off the ground.

Magnus settles his headset over his ears and asks, "Where the hell are we going?"

"The estate."

"Oh, good. I miss that damn dog."

Before I can ask him what the hell he's talking about, I'm distracted by the flames and heat barreling down the mountain like a runaway train.

This is bad. Really bad.

Magnus points to the sky, darkened by thick clouds of smoke and flying ash. "Gonna storm in a few hours. Hopefully, there's still something left to be saved by the time it starts."

LINCOLN

"Aren't we stopping at your house?" Whitney asks as we fly toward the estate.

"Why?"

"Your stuff!"

I reach out and squeeze her hand. "It's wood, glass, and rock. The only thing that truly matters is right here by my side."

"Ain't that sweet." Magnus's voice comes over the headset, reminding me that the old man can hear everything we say.

"Hopefully, it doesn't get this far," Whitney says, and I know we're all hoping the same thing. But I was telling the truth. As long as I have her, everything else can be replaced.

When we reach the estate, instead of seeing the driveway full of cars lined up and the staff scurrying around, loading them with valuables and antiques, there's no movement.

"What the hell?"

The chopper lands on the helipad, and I'm on the ground as quickly as Whitney was at Magnus's place.

"Stay here," I yell to them as I run toward the house and the rotors begin to slow.

When I open the front door, I expect complete chaos inside, but instead there's . . . eerie silence. Until I hear Commodore's voice boom from the library.

"Over my dead body."

"That can be arranged, old man."

The second voice is unmistakable. My brother.

What the hell is going on?

I creep toward the door to the library, and with every step, foreboding curls around my spine.

"Sign it, or I'll make sure this house burns down around you. Did you know they say burning alive is the worst pain a human can suffer?"

What the fuck?

I reach the door, and a peek inside reveals Harrison standing over Commodore, a pistol trained on my grandfather and a stack of documents in front of him.

"You shot my fucking dog. You really think I'm going to sign a goddamn thing? If you had a brain in your head, you'd already realize I have exactly one answer for you. Go fuck yourself, boy."

"Shut your fucking mouth, old man. I've had enough of your lectures. *Fucking years of them.* I was never good enough. Smart enough. Fast enough. Nothing was ever fucking enough for you! Now, pick up the fucking pen and sign your goddamn name on that line, or I swear to Christ I'll make sure you die as painfully as you deserve."

Commodore leans back in his chair and crosses his good arm over his sling. "If you'd shown even a fraction of this much conviction or devotion to something that mattered, we probably wouldn't be in this position."

"I told you to shut the fuck up and sign it!"

Harrison's face contorts with rage, mottled and red. His hair sticks up in different directions like he's run his hands through it over and over, probably as he cursed our grand-father—while holding a gun on him.

And I'm empty-handed.

"No way in hell. I'd rather burn. And even if I did, no one would believe I'd leave you everything. They all know me—and you—better than that."

Harrison's arm straightens and he lowers the gun. But instead of putting it down, a shot cracks and Commodore yelps in pain, clutching his leg with his good hand.

"You motherfucking, piss-ant piece of shit! You shot me!"

My grandfather sags forward in his power chair, and more than anything right now, I wish I had a gun.

My brother shot my grandfather and his dog.

"You should've listened to me. You shouldn't have been such a bastard to my mother. You know what? She'd be clapping right now and cheering me on. She hated you too. And not to have a funeral for her? What kind of dick move is that? She deserved better, you asshole. She deserved the best. You insulted her in life and in death, and now I'm going to take my revenge and hers."

My brother sounds like a demented movie villain, and I step away from the door, intent on getting to the study where the gun safe is located. But I step on a board that creaks, and both men's heads whip in my direction.

"Oh . . . this is too perfect. I don't even have to come looking for you. I can take out two for the price of one."

The barrel of Harrison's gun levels on me. "I've been waiting for you to come rushing in like the hero you think you are. I heard the fucking helicopter. Couldn't miss your grand entrance. Why don't you step right inside, big brother? After all, this affects you too. Not that it's going to matter that you won't be inheriting shit, because you're going to die now too."

He drops his gaze to Commodore. "If you don't sign that goddamn paper, I'm going to kill him right in front of you, and I hope you enjoy watching your golden boy bleed out next to your damn dog."

Commodore's sharp brown gaze bores into me. "Run."

Harrison lashes out, pistol-whipping him in the temple. The old man's head drops forward and his body goes limp.

"What the fuck are you doing, Harrison?"

My brother's smile turns evil. "Getting what I deserve. I've waited long enough, and I'm done. If there's one thing I learned from you and the old man, it's that you have to go after what you want. You can't sit around and wait for it to come to you."

"Call 911, right the fuck now. Commodore needs paramedics."

Harrison laughs. "Nah, he's not dying. Not until he signs his brand-new will that leaves everything to the oldest surviving descendant." Harrison's gaze turns bright and shiny. "Which will be me, as soon as you're out of the way. Sorry, brother, but this was never going to end well for you."

"Are you fucking insane? What the hell is wrong with you?" I snap out the questions, and I'm dead serious. There's nothing about Harrison's actions that include even a hint of sanity.

"No, Lincoln. I'm fucking fed up. Some people come and shoot up their old office—well, I'm doing it a little different. I'm going to burn it all down and walk the fuck away from here with all the insurance money."

His comment catches me off guard. "You started the fire? On purpose?"

Harrison's proud smile makes me sick. "Ten out of ten for creative tactics, am I right? I inherit everything, and that everything isn't a bunch of fucking trees in the ground in this shit-hole town. No, instead I get cash, and I can walk away and start over far away from anyone who has ever heard the name Riscoff."

I'm still trying to find words to respond when someone else speaks from beside me.

"Not so fast, boy."

A shot rings out, and Harrison screams as he drops to his knees. "My hand!"

Commodore's head lolls to the side as what's left of Harrison's mangled hand spills blood onto the carpet. His pistol lies a foot away from him, his fingers still attached.

"I'll kill you, old man!"

Harrison dives for his gun with his left hand, but I'm across the room quicker than he can move as he bleeds. I kick the gun away before he can reach it, and it slides across the carpet and spins on the wood floor. As soon as my fingers grasp the blood-slick metal, I whip around to face him.

Before I have to make the choice of whether to shoot my brother, Magnus Gable walks into the room, his rifle raised and sighted in on Harrison's head.

"Now, what the fuck is going on here?"

WHITNEY

WHEN THE GUNSHOT RANG OUT, Magnus was out of the chopper with impressive speed. I followed on his heels into the house, terror charging through my system.

There was no way in hell I was going to get Lincoln back, and have his ring on my finger, just to lose him now.

No. Fucking. Way.

When we cleared the threshold and I heard Harrison's yelling, the knot in my stomach twisted into something unrecognizable. I remembered how he destroyed everything he could touch on the way out. I remembered what a spoiled, entitled brat he was.

And I knew he'd come back for revenge.

Magnus acted before I could even begin to comprehend what I was seeing play out in front of me. Now he's standing over Harrison, the rifle barrel inches from his head, while Lincoln holds a pistol dripping with blood. Commodore's head hangs forward in his power chair, which is pushed in front of a table.

"You little pussy prick," Magnus says as he looms over

Harrison. "You shot Goose! He was a good goddamn dog. What the hell is wrong with you, you sick fuck?"

"He also started the fire," Lincoln says.

"What? Why?" I ask.

"I'll explain later. Call 911. They both need an ambulance."

"The chopper will be quicker," Magnus says. "But I'd let that brother of yours burn in the fire of his own making. I call that poetic justice."

"You fucking—"

"I will end you, boy. Don't say another goddamn word." Magnus pushes the barrel against Harrison's forehead to shut him up. "I'll make a hell of a mess at this range."

"Don't kill the boy. Even if he isn't my grandson . . . I don't need that on my conscience." Commodore's words are slurred and slow, but clear enough for us all to understand.

"What?" Lincoln snaps out the question, the gun in his hand wavering.

"He's not your father's son."

"You fucking knew! She told me you didn't!" Harrison ignores Magnus's order. He holds his arm against his chest, blood pouring from what's left of his hand. The color is already draining from his face, and I might not know shit about shit, but I'm guessing he's going to bleed out if we don't get him help, and fast.

"Everyone to the chopper. The police can meet us at the hospital," Lincoln says.

Magnus lowers his rifle. "Piece of shit. Doesn't surprise me you're not a Riscoff. At least they've got balls." He reaches for the handles on the back of

185

Commodore's power chair. "Let's get the hell out of here before you're even more useless than you are already in this damn chair."

With blood trickling down his forehead, Commodore half laughs, half groans. "You're lucky you didn't hit me with that shot, with how your hand shakes. Could've killed me."

"Then who would I hassle on a daily basis? Pissing you off is the only thing keeping me alive at this point."

LINCOLN

WHEN I DROPPED to my knees to lift Goose's body and carry him out of the house, Commodore ordered me to leave him. His exact words were, "If the house burns, it's a fitting funeral pyre for a damn good dog."

For the first time in years, a tear trickled down my grandfather's face as Magnus wheeled him away.

Harrison kept up his tirade until he lost consciousness, and the entire chopper flight was a blur of smoke and ash and disbelief.

When we land at the hospital, cops and an emergency crew meet us on the front lawn. Commodore and Harrison are both wheeled inside on stretchers, with the cops beside Harrison's, per my orders.

A lone photographer snaps pictures as we make our way into the hospital. Thunder booms overhead, and the sky is black from ash and smoke.

Whitney tilts her face skyward. "Please, let it rain."

I echo her plea silently, because the last thing we need is for the fire to make it all the way into town.

The fire my brother set.

My brother who isn't my full brother. Yet another family secret that's been kept from me my whole life.

One more secret that doesn't matter right now.

As soon as we make it into the ER waiting room, the sheriff stops me. "You want to explain to me what the hell is going on, and why we've got a man on your brother like he's some kind of criminal?"

"Not here." I glance around at the curious faces of the people in the waiting room. "Somewhere private. But yes, keep a man on him."

Whitney looks toward the elevator, and I know what she's thinking. She needs to check on Jackie and Cricket and get an update on Karma's surgery.

I squeeze her hand. "Go on up. I'll be here."

"Are you sure?"

"We divide and conquer."

She wraps her arms around me and hugs me hard. "I'm so sorry about your brother. I—"

"I know. We'll handle it just like we handle everything else. As a team." I kiss her forehead. "Now go. Your aunt and cousin need you."

"You're my rock. Thank you for holding me together through all of this."

"That's what I'm here for. I love you."

As soon as I release my hold on her and Whitney walks away, I feel the loss of her. She's my rock as much as I am hers. She may not realize it, but she holds me together as effectively as I do her.

This is what it's supposed to be like, I think as she walks away. It's not simply the crazy chemistry of our forbidden affair ten years ago. It's something better. Something deeper. Something real enough to sustain a lifetime of hardships and allow us both to come out the other side whole, because we truly are stronger together than we are apart.

And nothing will stop me from marrying her. Not even my brother, who planned to kill me.

Bile rises in my throat, but I tap into my remaining reserves of strength and walk through the ER doors to find my brother and my grandfather and figure out what the fuck we're going to do now.

I still can't believe he did all of this . . . just for money

If I hadn't experienced it myself, I wouldn't believe it. And even now, I still don't know how to comprehend it.

I find Commodore in a private treatment room being fussed over by doctors, with Magnus Gable sitting in the corner. I always wondered if their constant fighting was really part of a friendship they didn't want to admit to having, even to themselves. From the way Magnus watches him, concern lining his weathered face, I think it's a safe conclusion to draw.

"Sir, do you have a preference on surgeons? We'll need to make sure there's no—"

"Is surgery going to make me walk again?" Commodore asks, cutting the doctor off.

Even pale from blood loss caused by the gunshot to his leg and being hit in the head, my grandfather still appears as strong as ever. This is the second time he's been shot in a week, and to look at the stubborn set of his chin, you wouldn't realize it.

They don't make men like my grandfather anymore. Men who can take hit after hit and laugh in the face of whoever thinks it's possible to destroy them. Not even losing the ability to walk after having his legs crushed in a logging accident fazed him. He may be ruthless, but he loves his family fiercely and is the most ferociously loyal person I've ever met. The only time I've seen him come close to breaking was when my grandmother died. I remember what he said that day as clearly as if it were yesterday.

"They don't make women like her anymore."

He was wrong. They do. Whitney Gable is a woman just like that, and I will cherish her every day that we have together. My grandfather may not be a saint, but I could do worse than to follow his example in many ways.

One of the doctors sputters a response to Commodore's question. "Well, no. Sir, you know that we tried everything we could to make that happen, but—"

Commodore waves him off. "Then there's no reason I need to have surgery if it's not going to work any miracles."

"We would still suggest, in the interest of ruling out any possible complications from the gunshot wound—"

"No. You said the bullet went through. My knee is already busted. No point in wasting time or resources if it's not gonna fix the damn thing."

I cross the room to stand at my grandfather's bedside. "If you'll excuse us, we'll discuss this. I'm sure you have plenty of other patients to see, as long as my grandfather is stable for now."

The three doctors look at me, and I read relief on all their faces. One speaks up, taking the role of team leader.

"Yes, sir. But surgery would still be his best option to rule out any possible complications. Gunshot wounds in that area can be very difficult. Although, he's right . . . surgery isn't going to enhance his mobility at all."

"Thank you for the information. We'll discuss it and get back to you shortly."

They nod and leave the room. As soon as the door closes behind them, I sit in the chair next to my grandfather's bedside.

"What the fuck happened?"

"That's what I want to know," Magnus says from the corner.

Commodore's gaze, a little glassy from the painkillers he's no doubt been given, meets mine. "I always knew that entitled little prick would finally snap. Now the whole goddamn town's at risk because he threw a temper tantrum. I gotta buy Magnus a bottle of his favorite Scotch to thank him for stopping the little asshole from shooting me."

"Damn right, you do. I'll take some Glenlivet. The fifty-year-old single malt."

Commodore grunts out a laugh. "You'll get your Scotch, old man. As soon as I'm not doped up on whatever the hell they gave me. Now, give us some goddamn privacy so I can talk to my grandson."

Magnus harrumphs from the corner. "I'm gonna find out all of it anyway, but I'll go find you some tar they pass off as coffee in this place."

"Black. None of that Equal shit you like to put in yours."

"Like I don't know how you take your coffee, Riscoff. You want anything, kid?" Magnus asks me.

I shake my head, not only to say no, because it's clear

these two have been friends for longer than I could have guessed. "Thank you, Magnus."

As the most senior Gable walks out of the treatment room, I look at my grandfather. There are a hundred questions I want to ask him right now, but I start with the one that's confusing me the most.

"What did you mean when you said Harrison wasn't a Riscoff?"

Commodore's lips press together. "I shouldn't have said anything. I should've let it die with your mother." His dark gaze turns sharp. "But blood always tells."

"You're saying my mother had an affair . . . and Harrison was the product of that affair?"

Lead settles in my gut when he nods. My brain spins with the confirmation, and I can't help but think of how often I thought she showed her favoritism with my brother. How she protected him when my father would turn the nasty side of his temper on Harrison.

Wait . . . "Did my father know?"

A vivid memory comes back, when I was ten and Harrison was still using training wheels on his bike. My father ridiculed him for it and said that a Riscoff would be able to ride a bike without them already.

He had to have known.

Commodore shrugged. "I think he assumed, but there wasn't much he could say. He was off fucking around with God only knows who for most of his marriage to Sylvia."

Except his marriage to my mother wasn't valid because he was already married to Renee Rango, and the lawyer never filed the damn divorce papers.

Our family history will never be anything but muddy,

but I keep slogging through it. "Who is Harrison's father then?"

My grandfather lays his head back against the white pillow. At least his color seems to be coming back. "Does it really matter?"

"I think we've all kept enough secrets to last a lifetime at this point."

"Some lawyer that worked for the company for a while. He came out to the house a few times and caught your mother's eye. He got fired shortly after for screwing something up, and went back to the city to find another job."

It's almost impossible to imagine my mother having an affair, but like I just said to Commodore, we've all kept enough secrets to last a lifetime. At this point, there isn't much that would surprise me.

"How did you find out?"

His gaze narrows. "I know everything, boy. People might pretend they're good at keeping secrets, but something always slips. You just have to know the signs."

I glance toward the door that Whitney's great-uncle walked out. "I saw the signs about you and Magnus Gable being friends, but the fact that you were bleeding because he shot at you threw me off."

Commodore grins. "It was all in good fun. Just another upside of moving out of the estate. Not getting poisoned, and I needed some entertainment in my life. Gable makes damn good coffee too."

Against all odds, my shoulders shake with laughter. "I'm glad you found something to keep you entertained."

"If our places get burned down, he and I are both rebuilding. We're too old to start over anywhere else."

"I'll make you a deal, Commodore. If you let the doctors take care of you, I'll make sure there's a path built for your chair between the two cabins."

"Maybe."

I decide to count that as a victory, and move on to the more important question of the day.

"What the hell are we going to do about Harrison?"

WHITNEY

I FIND MY AUNT, my brother, Cricket, and Hunter all upstairs in a private surgical waiting room. I'm not even sure how the hell I'm going to explain what happened, but when I walk in and see Jackie in a seat beside Asa, her arms wrapped around herself and Cricket's head lying on her shoulder, I know they don't care about Harrison Riscoff right now.

"How is Karma doing? Did you get an update?"

Jackie looks up and tears pool in her blue eyes. "They found more than they thought when they opened her up. They're trying to get everything they can, but—" She breaks off into a sob.

Cricket meets my gaze. "They have to do a full hysterectomy. Karma won't be able to have any more kids." Hunter reaches out to take her hand and squeeze.

"But . . . but she's going to make it? They're going to be able to get all the cancer?"

Tears roll down Jackie's face. "They don't know. It spread. She should've gone to the goddamn doctor instead of waiting. She could've gotten help sooner, and it wouldn't have gotten so bad. Instead, it's just been spreading."

That doesn't sound good on any level.

"But she's going to be fine, right?" I ask again because I need to understand exactly what we're dealing with here.

"They're trying." Asa stands and comes toward me to wrap an arm around my shoulders. "They're doing their best."

"When will we know?"

"Soon. We hope," Jackie says, and I walk over to give her a hug. My aunt's strong and capable frame feels frailer than I've ever felt, and I hate that all of this is taking a massive toll on her.

When Jackie retakes her seat, Asa pulls me away from them, his gaze locked on the blood on my shirt. "What the hell happened out there?"

His tone screams *protective older brother*, and his stance says he's ready to go to battle. I can only imagine how pissed he was when he found out we left in the chopper to stage a rescue effort without him. With his military training, I'm sure he would have appointed himself team leader of the operation.

I give him the rundown, and he doesn't look nearly as stunned as I expect. "I'll kill that little bastard myself for starting the fucking fire. I've been watching the news and waiting on updates about Karma before I go offer my services to the evacuation effort. This shit needs to be organized or it'll turn into a complete clusterfuck."

"Where do they stand with the evacuation right now?"

"Half the town is on notice. If they're smart, everyone

on the other side of the river will get the fuck out as soon as possible."

"Are they evacuating The Gables yet?"

"If they're smart."

Jackie stands. "But Addy and Maddy are at The Gables."

Shit. How had I forgotten that?

"I'll have Lincoln talk to his sister. She can bring them—"

Before I can finish my sentence, a code is called over the hospital's PA system, and in the hallway, we hear someone swear and break into a run.

Confused, I look around the room. "What does that mean? What was that code?"

I have no idea how he knows, but Asa meets my gaze first.

"They're getting ready to evacuate the hospital."

LINCOLN

I GRAB an ER nurse as soon as the code is called and everyone outside the room breaks into a flurry of movement. "What the hell is going on?"

Her eyes wide, she says, "We have to evacuate."

Fuck.

Magnus just returned with coffee and curses under his breath. Commodore sits up in the hospital bed.

"Evacuate? Here?" I ask.

The woman nods, and I think of Whitney's family upstairs. "What about the people in surgery? What happens to them?"

"I assume they try to get them stable and then move them. I don't know anything else, sir. This has never happened in the time I've worked here. I'm so sorry."

"Find someone who's in charge. Send them in here."

She nods and scurries away, and I figure the chance of her actually following directions has dropped to slim-to-none as soon as she disappears into the chaos in the hallway.

"Fuck," I whisper, and turn to find Commodore shifting in the hospital bed. "What are you doing?"

"I gotta get the fuck out of this bed and back into my chair. I'm not helpless."

I look at his knee, which is bandaged. "Sir, they're going to come for you. Let me go find—"

"You think I survived the war by waiting for someone to come for me after my plane went down? No, I fucking broke out of that POW camp myself and made it back to my ship. Nothing good happens to those who wait. That's a load of bullshit. Now, wheel my chair over here and help me into it. I'm not burning to death in this building when someone forgets about me."

"He's right." Magnus moves the chair across the room toward the bed. "I wouldn't wait either. We get him out now."

I can't fault their logic, because with the sudden onset of mass hysteria that has already taken hold of the hospital, there's no telling what could happen next. People in the halls are screaming to be moved, and the staff is no doubt going to be working as hard and quickly as possible.

This is everyone's worst nightmare, and Commodore already escaped being burned alive once today—at least, that was part of my brother's threat.

We help him into his chair, and I turn to Magnus. "They're probably going to evacuate down to Rock Hollow, unless somehow the fire changed direction. Wait for instructions, but if shit goes sideways, get the fuck out of here any way you can."

"We know what to do, boy," Commodore says. "Don't worry about us. Go get your woman and her family, and then we can talk about that wedding of yours I want to see happen."

My gaze snaps to his, and for a moment, I wonder if he's high on painkillers. "Excuse me, sir?"

"I think we all agree it's time to end this feud for good," he says as Magnus nods. "And that's how we're going to do it. We bring the families together and it'll be done."

"I agree," Magnus says. "Especially because you're not a little bitch like your brother."

Shaking my head, I glance from one lined face to the other. A Gable and a Riscoff. *Friends.* It sounds like the feud was already well on its way to ending, but no one told the rest of us yet. I think back to how Commodore told me to marry anyone but Whitney Gable when she first returned to town, and even though now is not the time to be discussing this, I ask one question.

"What changed your mind?"

Commodore's canny stare sparkles. "I've always liked her. She's got spunk and heart. Your grandmother would've approved. Now, go get that girl and her people, and let's get the hell out of here. Tell them we're paying for all the transport if they need extra incentive to move that cousin of hers more quickly."

I reach out and grasp my grandfather's good hand. "Thank you."

"No time for the sentimental shit. We've got a hospital to clear." He squeezes my hand and then reaches for the control on his power chair. "In case I didn't say it before, I'm proud of you, boy. Damn proud. You grew up to be a hell of a good man who anyone could rely on."

From the look on his face, I know he's telling me the

absolute truth. Commodore Riscoff may not be a perfect man, by any stretch of the imagination, but he's one of the best I've known. Under his influence, I became the man I am today. I've battled with being able to trust anyone, but Whitney finally broke down those walls.

Maybe I was missing the point of that lesson all along. It isn't that trusting others is bad, but that you have to be able to trust yourself first and be strong enough for others to depend on.

Commodore took a legacy and turned it into an empire, and he gave me all the tools to do the same.

"Thank you, sir."

With one nod at Commodore, I head for the hallway to find Whitney.

I make it only a handful of steps before coming to a dead stop in front of a doorway where someone is yelling. Someone whose voice I recognize. I look inside to see my brother, whose mangled hand is wrapped with bandages, yanking at the cuff hooking his good hand to the bed as he screams for someone to unlock him.

"You better not let me burn here, you fucking idiots. My family will take every single penny this hospital has ever made if anything happens to me."

Harrison's ridiculous threats stop the moment he sees me. His lips curl, and he glares.

"You think this is funny, big brother? You think you finally won? Go fuck yourself. You haven't won shit."

It's entirely possible that my brother has lost his goddamned mind, but I don't have time to worry about that. Hundreds of lives are at risk right now—thousands, if you count the town—and Harrison has proven he has zero respect for the sanctity of human life.

"Shut up, Harrison. You're a disgrace, and you don't deserve the Riscoff name. They'll move you when they move you."

He yanks at the cuff. "You're going to leave me here, aren't you? You want me gone. You've always wanted me gone."

I take another step toward him and meet his gaze—one that looks like my mother's, but nothing like mine or McKinley's, but it never occurred to me to question it. Yet another thing that doesn't matter right now.

"It would be poetic justice if you died in the fire of your own making. *You* did this. No one else."

"But—"

"No. You don't get to speak until I tell you that you can speak."

Harrison's nostrils flare with rage, and I step toward him again, my fists clenched at my sides.

"I don't think you understand how much damage and destruction you've caused. When this is all over, every single penny of your trust fund and every dime in your bank account is going to go toward replacing what you've destroyed. *You did this.* You're responsible. No one else. You can try to blame everyone else like you have for everything in your goddamned life, but there's no arguing this. It's on you."

"You think you're so fucking perfect? You're—"

I turn and walk away from my brother's venom-charged words, not giving a single fuck what he has to say right now. He can scream down the halls for all I care.

As I walk away, I see a nurse. "Make sure Harrison Riscoff doesn't receive any special treatment in the evacuation process. In fact, make sure you get every single patient out of here before you even think about moving him. You understand me?"

"Fuck you, Lincoln!" Harrison yells from the room, as he no doubt overhears my order. "You can't let me burn!"

The nurse's eyes go wide. "Excuse me, sir?"

"Ignore him. You heard me. Harrison Riscoff goes last. Everyone else goes first. He set this fire, and I won't let him try to use my family's name to escape the consequences of it."

Shocked, she nods at the order.

I leave the ER, the sound of Magnus Gable's voice in my ears as he helps Commodore down the hall.

"Come on, cripple. Let's get you the hell out of here."

I can't help but smile as I dash up the stairs.

WHITNEY

PURE CHAOS. That's the only way I can describe what's happening right now.

A nurse comes to the waiting room and tells us that all family and visitors have to leave immediately, and that they will be able to meet their loved ones at the hospital in Rock Hollow, which is where they're temporarily being moved.

"But what about my daughter? She's in surgery. I'm not going anywhere until I know she's okay," Jackie protests.

The nurse is completely no-nonsense with her. "Ma'am, I know you're concerned, but right now, the best thing you can do for your daughter is make sure that you're waiting for her when she gets to Rock Hollow. You won't be allowed to travel with her. We've got too many patients to move, and every county within a hundred miles has ambulances on the way here to assist."

"Is there anything we can do?" Asa asks. "Help move patients? Transport them?"

I don't know if it's the tone of his voice or his posture that clues her in to the fact that he has military experience, but the nurse surveys my brother differently.

"You can come with me, sir. We could use an extra pair of hands, if you're willing and able."

"I'd be happy to help any way I can."

Asa and the nurse leave the room, and Cricket, Hunter, and I watch Jackie as she paces and shoves her hands through her hair.

"I'm not leaving this hospital without my baby. I'm not doing it."

"Mom—" Cricket says, and Aunt Jackie whips around to face her and Hunter.

"Call Ms. Gable and get Addy and Maddy. Take them to the hospital at Rock Hollow, and God forbid, if the winds change, you get them out of harm's way. That's your only job right now."

"Yes, ma'am. That's exactly what I was going to suggest," Hunter says.

Cricket nods. "Okay. We're going." She gives me a quick hug, and then she and Hunter disappear through the doorway.

As soon as they're gone, I try to talk Aunt Jackie down from her panicked state.

"You heard the nurse. The best thing we can do is get out of the way. They don't need to be worrying about anyone who isn't a patient. So let's go, and help anyone we can on the way out."

She spins around and looks at me. "I know you and Karma don't get along. She doesn't get along much with anyone, but she's still my child. I won't abandon her."

The steel in her tone and the implacable determination

in her eyes tell me that I won't be able to convince my aunt Jackie of anything right now, especially leaving this hospital without knowing Karma has already been evacuated. But that doesn't stop me from trying.

"What about waiting in the parking lot? You can watch for her to be moved, and then we follow the ambulance convoy all the way to Rock Hollow. There's no reason to stay inside and wait now."

She spears me with a stare. "You go. Make sure Magnus is okay. Find Lincoln. Wait for us at the other hospital. I'll meet you there with Karma."

"Jackie—"

She shakes her head. "It doesn't matter what you say to me right now. I'm not leaving this room until she's out of surgery and they have a plan to move her. You need to go, Whitney. Don't wait for me."

"I'm not leaving this hospital without you, Jackie. I'll give you a little time to get confirmation on how and when they're going to move Karma, but you better be ready to go when I come back for you. Because if I have to drag you out kicking and screaming, I will."

My aunt nods.

I wish I could believe she's agreeing with me and not just trying to get me to go, but I don't buy it for a second. Making a promise to myself that I will come back for her as soon as I find Lincoln, I leave the room.

I reach into my pocket for my phone so I can text Lincoln to find out where he is . . . but it's gone. *Shit.* I have no idea when I lost it, but there's a good chance it's either in the chopper or somewhere on the lawn of the Riscoff estate. Either way, it won't help me.

The hallway is an obstacle course of IV poles, patients

in beds and wheelchairs, and hospital staff trying to stay organized in the face of chaos. I can barely find my way through the maze of everyone desperate to get the hell out of here with the fire closing in. I catch snippets of conversation with every other person I dodge.

"They say it's moving fast. Wind's picked up."

"The whole town might burn."

"It's worse than the blaze back in 1901."

"If we don't hurry, we might not make it out in time."

"They better save an ambulance for me. I can't walk."

Fear tinges everyone's tone, and I wish there was something I could do to offer comfort. But right now, it sounds like the best thing I can do is get the hell out of the way.

I find a stairwell and jog down two flights to the bottom, intent on finding Lincoln and figuring out how to get the hell out of here as fast as possible, with all the people we love.

He has a helicopter. There's no reason they can't transport Karma in that. My aunt would definitely leave then. When I see Lincoln, that's going to be the first thing I ask him.

Except I can't get to the ER because the hallway is completely blocked.

Shit.

I turn around to retrace my steps, but instead of heading up the stairs again, I have a different idea. If I can get out of the hospital, I can come around the side to get back in through the front to the ER that way. I turn down the hallway that leads toward radiology, which is already completely empty, and scan for the nearest exit.

I spot the red letters on the sign and lock onto it like a

beacon. I dart toward it, but a body slams into me from the side.

Like an idiot, my first instinct is to apologize. "Sorry, I was—"

"Fucking up my entire goddamned life because you just couldn't stay away." Harrison Riscoff's face, contorted in a mask of rage, is inches from mine.

I blink in shock, my attention shifting to the white bandage wrapped around his hand and a sling holding it close to his body. He's still wearing his blood-spattered shirt from earlier.

"But you're gonna stay gone this time," he says, spittle flying from his lips and pupils the size of pinpricks.

Where the hell did he come from? Lincoln told the deputy to have someone stay with him.

I jerk my head around, intending to look for the cop he must have slipped away from, but there's no one in the hall. Just us.

Harrison lifts his good hand, which is wrapped around the grip of a pistol.

Oh sweet Jesus. No.

"Harrison, please just—"

"Don't tell me what the fuck to do. I'm the one with the gun, you Gable bitch."

His good hand jerks, but instead of pulling the trigger, he slams the butt of the gun into my temple.

Stars burst in my field of vision and pain radiates out from where he connected. I wobble on my feet before everything starts to fade into darkness.

"That's right, bitch. You're going to sleep, and you're never waking up again."

LINCOLN

I find Jackie Gable alone in the surgical waiting room.

"Where did Whitney go? Why aren't you evacuating?"

Whitney's aunt spins to stare at me. "I'm not leaving until Karma is out of surgery."

"Please, Jackie. Wait outside. Whitney will never forgive me if I leave you here."

Jackie's lips flatten. "She already tried to get me to go. I'll tell you exactly what I told her—I'm waiting."

"We have a chopper outside to evacuate Karma. Okay?"

Her face relaxes for a beat and then tenses again. "They have to finish the surgery first. *She could die.*"

"We'll get her out of here alive. I promise." It's not a promise I should be making, but I do it anyway.

Jackie nods. "Okay. I'll come out after I get another update. They should be coming any moment."

"Good. Now, where the hell is Whitney?"

Jackie points toward the door. "She left to find you."

Shit.

"Okay. Then I'll go back to the ER, find her, and we'll meet you at the chopper. Got it?"

"Got it."

I can't waste another moment hoping Jackie is telling me the truth rather than just telling me what I want to hear. I need to find Whitney.

But when I make it back to the ER, there's no sign of her. I stop in front of my brother's room and find the bed empty but for a pile of sheets.

I step inside, shocked to see a nurse lying passed out next to the bed. The sheriff's deputy is crumpled on the floor beside her.

Fuck.

I drop to a knee beside the woman and shake her. She doesn't wake up, and the deputy's blood pools beneath them both.

"Help! I need some fucking help in here!"

My bellow carries over the cacophony of noise in the ER, and within moments, someone drops to their knees beside me. One of the ER docs who was with Commodore.

"Jesus Christ. What the hell happened?"

"I have no idea," I tell him.

He feels for a pulse on the nurse and then the deputy. "He's breathing, but she barely is. Fucking Christ."

I spy a syringe on the floor a few feet away and scramble over to pick it up. "Could she have been drugged?"

I hold it up and the doctor looks at it and then to the bed.

"This was your brother's room, right? He was restrained?"

I nod. "Yeah, but he's clearly not anymore." I look at

the deputy's belt. He's missing his service weapon. "And now he's armed and fucking dangerous."

"We have to get them both out of here," the doctor says. "Everyone has to go. They say the wind's picked up and shifted, putting us directly in the path of the wildfire if it crosses the river, which they're predicting it will. It'll take us a couple more hours to evacuate the hospital, and the forest service told us we need to be out in ninety minutes."

This is the first I've heard of a specific timeline, and the gravity of the situation hits me hard.

"What can I do to help?"

"Find me some help. I need to stabilize both of them before we can get them out of here."

"Got it." I pause at the doorway. "What about the surgeries in progress? What if they can't be wrapped up in time?"

The doctor looks at me, his expression grim. "They don't have a choice, unless they all want to die." He turns away from me and opens a drawer to pull out supplies.

As soon as I step out of the room, I grab the first medical professional I see. "Doc needs you. In there. Please."

The woman's brows dip together. "But I'm—"

"Please," I repeat. "He's trying to work on two patients who were attacked, and he needs help."

"Yes, sir."

As she rushes into the room, I yank my phone from my pocket and call my office. One of the assistants answers the phone.

"Is everyone evacuating?" I ask in lieu of a greeting.

"Yes, sir. Everyone's out of the building and loading up their cars."

"Tell them to stop at the hospital on the way out of town. We've got people who need rides."

She goes quiet. "You want us to . . ."

"Send every single person with an open seat to the hospital, right now. We need all the help we can get. Otherwise, these people will be trapped here."

"Yes, sir. I'll spread the word."

My next call is to my sister.

"Thank God, Lincoln. I just heard from Cricket Gable. Is it true Harrison started the fire?"

"Yes, but we can't talk about it now. Are the kids safe?"

"Yes, we're in the Escalade, headed to Rock Hollow. Cricket and Hunter are meeting me there."

"Good. Keep those kids safe. Don't stop for anyone. Understand me?"

"Yes, of course. If Rock Hollow isn't safe enough, we'll keep going."

"I love you, Mac. We're going to get through this."

"I love you too, Linc. And I know we will. We're Riscoffs."

I hang up with her, wondering how the hell I'm going to tell her that Harrison isn't our full brother, and then decide it doesn't matter right now.

I wouldn't care if McKinley wasn't my full sister. Although, given that she looks exactly like our paternal grandmother, I'd find that hard to believe.

Regardless, there'll be plenty of time to worry about this later when everyone I love is safe and accounted for— and right now, I have no fucking clue where Whitney is.

I charge into the stream of people rushing out the front of the hospital and look everywhere I can for her black hair. I rush from one group to another, asking if anyone has seen her, but no one has.

Where the hell are you, Whitney? I won't fucking lose you now.

WHITNEY

I FIGHT the wave of blackness that washes over me, but Harrison hit me hard. I keep blinking and try to focus, but I can't.

Suddenly, I'm shoved forward and my hips ram into something metal. My feet are picked up off the floor, and I land facedown on something soft. *A gurney?*

Wheels squeak as we start to move. No, not move. *Roll.*

What the hell? Where is he taking me?

"What are you . . ." I try to roll over, but my body doesn't want to cooperate, and my brain stumbles when I speak.

"Shut the fuck up, whore. My brother never should've fucking touched your skank ass."

His words echo, and there's no sound from any other hospital staff or patients. *Where is he taking me?*

When he pushes the gurney around a corner, I finally manage to roll over and struggle to sit up. The hallway we're in is completely empty.

This area must have already been evacuated?

Before I can come to any conclusions, Harrison stops to land another solid blow to my temple. Again, white stars burst in my field of vision, but I know I can't give in to the darkness that's trying to take me under.

If I pass out, I'm going to die. I know it.

And that's not going to fucking happen. I bite down on my lower lip, and the jolt of pain keeps my eyes open.

I'm not dying today. I have too much to live for. Lincoln and our life and our future.

Something cold closes over my wrist with a metallic click. The sound repeats, but it's metal on metal the second time.

Handcuffs.

I jerk against the metal, but my hand is trapped.

He handcuffed me to a gurney. Fucking hell.

"I would just shoot you, but it'll be way better knowing you're going to burn alive for what you did to my mother, you cunt."

He shoves the gun in his waistband and pulls open a door with his good hand.

I twist around to see shelves of linens behind me as Harrison pushes the gurney inside with his hip.

"No!" I scream, and the word echoes down the empty hallway.

"There's no one to hear you scream, whore."

I open my mouth to yell again, but a shriek fills the air.

"I heard her, you asshole!"

Harrison whips around, still in the hallway, and the next thing I see makes me wonder if I'm hallucinating.

My aunt Jackie launches herself into the air, her hands outstretched, reaching for his throat.

Where the hell did she come from? Did they already move Karma?

Her fingers curl around his neck and they both hit the floor. I struggle toward the end of the gurney closest to the doorway.

"Jackie! He has a gun!"

I don't know where Harrison finds the strength, but he uses his one good hand to tear Jackie's fingers from his throat.

"Bitch!"

He flips onto his side like he's got superhuman strength, and Jackie's body smacks the floor. I yank at the cuff, trying to get to my aunt to help her battle this bastard, not caring at all that my wrist screams in pain.

I can't let him hurt her. I won't let him hurt her.

Harrison scrambles to his feet faster than Jackie can.

"No!" I yell, terrified about what he might do to my aunt next. "Stop! Help! Anyone!" I'm screaming like a crazy person and I don't even care. All I want is someone to stop Harrison before he can hurt Jackie more.

Harrison grabs Jackie by the arm and yanks her up, dragging her toward the closet where I'm trapped. "I'll kill two Gables for the price of one. You're all whores. Every single one of you. You can both die to pay for what your family did to my mother!"

Jackie kicks out at him, but Harrison barely flinches. Whatever painkillers he's on must have him feeling unstoppable.

"Bitch!"

"No, you're the little bitch."

I have no idea how she got Harrison's gun, but Jackie's arm swings up and she aims the gun at Harrison's face.

"You think you know everything, you little prick? You don't know anything! Whitney never did a goddamn thing to your mother. You want to know who killed her? *I did.* I killed them *all.*"

Shock rips through me at Jackie's screamed confession, and Harrison's jaw drops.

"What the fuck are you talking about, bitch?"

Jackie wraps her other hand around the grip of the pistol to steady it. "I killed your mother, you piece of shit. *Me.* I gave her the drugs. She was going to destroy my family, and I wasn't going to let it happen."

"What?" I breathe out the question, and Jackie turns to look at me for a second.

"I'm so sorry, Whit. I never wanted you to know."

This can't be happening. Jackie didn't really kill Mrs. Riscoff. Did she?

Before I can process any of it, Harrison makes a move to grab the gun, and I scream. Jackie pulls the trigger and a shot explodes. My ears ring, and I cover one with my free hand.

Harrison falls to his knees, and Jackie stands over him.

"You're lying," Harrison says. I don't know where Jackie shot him, but his voice sounds strangled.

"I don't need to lie about anything. I slipped that bitter, angry excuse for a woman the rest of the fentanyl, and now you can see her in hell."

Oh my God. Oh my God. With my ears ringing and tears streaming down my face, I stare at Jackie as she aims the barrel of the gun at Harrison's body.

"This is for trying to kill me and my niece."

She pulls the trigger, and I scream again.

I can't believe what I'm hearing and seeing. I can't

believe any of it. My head pounds from the percussion of the shot, and my heart bleeds for the Riscoffs.

Aunt Jackie has to be lying. She has to be. How can what she said possibly be true? Because if she killed Mrs. Riscoff with fentanyl . . . what does that mean? Did she kill Ricky too?

When my aunt turns to face me, I barely recognize her. Her green shirt is splattered with blood and gore, and the triumph on her face terrifies me.

"Please tell me you made that all up for his sake. Please. Please, Jackie."

I beg my aunt because I don't know what else to do. This isn't the woman who cleaned me up after I crashed on my bike, and put Band-Aids on my skinned knees. This isn't the woman who treated me like her own daughter when my family fell apart. Jackie has always been my champion. My supporter. A rock for us all to lean on.

She can't be a murderer. It's not possible.

The glow of triumph on her face fades several degrees when she takes in my horrified expression. She closes her eyes for a beat and when she opens them, I'm staring at my aunt again.

"I'm sorry, sweet girl. I had to. Sylvia was willing to do anything to keep you and Lincoln apart. She was going to have someone kill you, Whit. I couldn't let her do that. Not to you." She pauses as tears trickle down her face. "I couldn't let her take you from us. So when she'd rather die than let a Gable marry her son . . . I knew that was the only way. One of the maids found the fentanyl left in one of the rooms, and I confiscated it. It sat in my drawer for months, and I forgot about it. But it was like the hand of God helping me protect you, Whit. I knew she wouldn't suffer."

"Oh my God."

"It was the only way," she repeats. "I would do anything to protect our family, Whitney. *Anything.*"

What she said to Harrison a few moments ago echoes in my brain. *"I killed them all."*

"What did you mean . . . you killed them all? Who else?" I can't believe I'm asking this question right now, but I have to know.

My aunt's face turns grave. "I should've told you everything that night. I should've told you how sorry I was. I didn't mean to kill them. I just couldn't save them."

Jackie's words send waves of confusion rocking through me.

"What are you talking about?"

Her tears flow faster. "I was driving Roosevelt Riscoff's car that night it went over the bridge. We were arguing."

Oh my God. Jackie was driving his car? Not my mother? For ten years, I've thought that my father hit Roosevelt Riscoff's car because Roosevelt and my mother were trying to run away together and my father was enraged.

But if Jackie was driving Roosevelt's car . . . "Why? Why were you driving his car?"

Her shoulders droop for a moment before she looks up at me. "Because I was the one who had an affair with him. Not your mom. And you need to know . . . Ricky wasn't a Riscoff. Renee lied to Roosevelt. She would've never given a DNA sample because she was scamming him for years. He just wouldn't listen."

"What?" I blink twice, and my head pounds. Nothing feels real.

Jackie swallows. "Everyone lied, sweet girl, including me. But I couldn't tell the truth either. Cricket and Karma are Riscoffs. Roosevelt got me pregnant when I was twenty years old. He threatened me. Told me he'd only pay if I never said anything to anyone. I took the money."

Sweet Jesus. It's like listening to Renee Rango tell her story, except . . . apparently she lied about that too? Confusion batters my brain, and I can't figure out how all the pieces fit together. It's too overwhelming.

"Why were you in his car that night? Were you still having an affair?"

She shakes her head, and her features turn to stone. Once more, I'm looking at a stranger.

"No. Once I told him I was pregnant, he never touched me again. I would've shot him first."

"I don't understand." I whisper the words, and it's the truth. How could she have been in his car that night if the affair had been over for twenty years?

"Roosevelt saw Karma in a bar. He hit on her, not realizing she was his daughter. When she came home and told me what happened, I lost it. *He hit on his own daughter. Who does that?*" Jackie's face contorts as she wails the words.

"Oh my God." I lift one hand to my mouth, pressing hard as though it can stop the bile rising in my throat. I feel like I'm going to be sick.

Jackie might sound crazy, but I know she has absolutely no reason to lie. Which means . . . *Cricket and Karma are Lincoln's half sisters. Roosevelt tried to hit on his own daughter. And somehow, Jackie is responsible for the accident that killed him and my parents.*

"What happened, Jackie? That night? My parents . . ." Tears burn rivers down my face as I beg her to tell me.

"I found Roosevelt at the bar, drunk. I dragged him out and put him in his car. I was taking him somewhere we could talk."

"And you drove over the bridge?"

She nods. "He was yelling at me, and he grabbed the wheel and we swerved into the other lane." She meets my gaze. "All I saw was headlights before we slammed into the other car, and we both went over the bridge."

There's so much information coming at me, I don't even know how to process it. Jackie keeps going.

"We hit the water, and everything happened so fast. I panicked. I wasn't going to die trying to save the man who propositioned his own daughter, so I left him in the car." Her shoulders shake.

"What about my parents? How could you leave them?"

"I saw the car go under. The river was moving so fast, I couldn't get to them. I almost drowned too. I didn't think I was going to make it out."

"You didn't even try to save them?"

She breaks down into sobs. "I couldn't. I'm so sorry, Whitney. It was all my fault. I never should have gone anywhere near Roosevelt Riscoff. They shouldn't even have been on the bridge that night, but your daddy went looking for your mom, thinking she was cheating, but instead he found her cleaning rooms at the Wham Bam Motel."

I remember the night my aunt showed up on my parents' doorstep, dripping wet, after Lincoln and I had gotten into a fight. I thought she was soaked from the rain

. . . but she'd been in the river, escaping the scene of the accident that killed my parents.

"But my mom . . . they said she swam to the bank somehow. That's why everyone thought she was driving Roosevelt's car. You let everyone think that!"

Jackie's already tortured expression twists. "I'm so sorry, Whit, so damned sorry. I've tried every day to protect you any way I could. I owed that to you. That's why I killed Ricky and Sylvia. I didn't want them to hurt you anymore."

My heart jumps into my throat.

"What? What did you say about Ricky?"

Jackie squeezes her eyes closed for a beat before looking up at me. "Cricket ran into the house crying after you called her from the safe room, saying he'd threatened you. I knew I had to do something, so I was on a flight within an hour. I found the party from the posts on the internet."

Oh my God. This can't be real. This can't be true. I listen in disbelief as Jackie continues.

"I sneaked inside, pretending to be part of the catering staff, and found Ricky. There were girls all over him. When one of them went to the bathroom, I told her I had some even better drugs for her to give him. She was too messed up to ask questions. That was the first time I used the fentanyl."

Even as horror at her confession rolls through me, I can picture the scene playing out in my head, as though I had been there myself. After all, I'd been to more parties with Ricky than I could count. It would have been a free-for-all with drugs everywhere. No one asks questions, except how they can get more. I always left as soon as things spiraled out of control.

"Then what happened?" I ask her.

Jackie shakes her head as she lowers the gun to the end of the gurney. "I left. I told myself if he decided not to do them, then it would be his own choice. But he did it. He put the needle in his veins. He killed himself."

My entire body prickles with goose bumps. She sounds like she's rationalizing her actions, but I don't know what to think anymore. Technically, she's right. She didn't force that needle into his veins. He made that choice. But . . .

"What about Sylvia?"

Jackie's expression turns hard. "I told you, she was making plans. She was talking to Maren about how she would take your place as soon as you were out of the way. Sylvia was never going to let you be with Lincoln. I slipped her the drugs in her tea. I would do it again. She would've never let you live happy, and that's all I've ever wanted for you, Whit. Just for you to live happy."

"Too . . . bad . . . you . . . have to die now too."

Harrison's strangled voice comes from below us, and Jackie screams as he knocks her off her feet and she crashes to the floor.

"No!" I shout, lunging forward only to be caught by the handcuff where he locked it on the rail.

On the floor, Harrison hammers at Jackie's face with his one good hand and his bloody stump before slamming her head into the floor over and over.

"Let her go!"

I grab the gun off the end of the bed, but there's no way I can shoot Harrison without hitting my aunt, so I do something else completely and utterly stupid.

I shoot my handcuff instead, shutting my eyes as I squeeze the trigger.

The percussion of the shot deafens me, but through some miracle, the metal chain connecting the bracelet to the frame snaps free. I vault toward the hallway where Jackie tries to crawl away from Harrison.

"Whitney?"

My brother's voice roars down the hallway as Harrison lashes out, catching me in the ankle. My feet go out from under me, and my head connects with the floor.

The last thing I hear before everything goes black is the sound of pounding footsteps and my brother's bellow as he drags Harrison away from us.

LINCOLN

ASA GABLE COMES out of the front of the hospital cradling two blood-spattered bodies against him, both with jet-black hair. When he lowers their dead weight to the ground, my heart practically stops.

"No!"

I run toward them, and the sight of Whitney's pale face sends fear like I've never known ripping through me.

I drop to my knees beside her. "What happened?"

When Whitney's brother meets my gaze, the gravity of his expression hits me even harder. "Your brother's dead. He tried to kill them both." Asa pauses. "I did what I had to do to save my family, and I won't apologize for it."

The thundering beat of a chopper's rotors almost drowns him out as it lands on the helipad, but I hear him clearly enough. My stomach drops to the ground beneath my feet.

This isn't how things were supposed to go. Waves of regret wash over me, but I pull myself together. I can grieve later.

"Where?"

"Back hallway on the first floor. Past radiology"

Someone speaks over a bullhorn before I respond. *"We need to evacuate the area as quickly as possible. We're down to one road, and it won't stay open long. Everyone must go now."*

Whitney stirs in the grass, her lids fluttering open to reveal her beautiful blue eyes. "Jackie? Where's Jackie?"

"She's right beside you, Whit," Asa says, crouching down to try to wake up their aunt.

"Where's Lincoln?"

"Right here."

Her blue gaze finds mine. "Harrison . . . he . . . he was going to kill us both. Jackie saved me. I'm so sorry. She had to shoot him."

I pull her against my body, and her shivers tear through me. "It's not your fault, Blue. It's not your fault."

"But I—"

"Stop. Not right now. Everything can wait. We have to get you somewhere safe."

"No. Not everything . . ."

Jackie Gable's voice, rough and ragged, interrupts as she regains consciousness. "I'm . . . I'm sorry. For everything I've done. I'm so sorry. I . . . I only wanted to protect my family . . ."

"Jackie, no!" Whitney cries as her aunt's body goes limp. Blood mats her hair, and her face is swelling from taking a beating. I don't have to ask to know that my brother did that to her. *And now he's dead.*

"No!" Whitney screams. "Someone help her!"

I lock down everything I'm feeling as I wrap Whitney in my arms and hold her as she sobs.

A doctor rushes over to Asa. "What's happening here?"

"I don't know, but we need help."

The doctor feels for a pulse. "She's still with us. We have one bus left. Bring her with me. Come on."

Asa lifts an unconscious Jackie into his arms and carries her to the last ambulance while I help Whitney to her feet.

"What about Karma? Where's Karma?" Whitney asks, coughing on the smoke that fills the air.

"Chopper took her to Rock Hollow. Surgical team went with her. The pilot's taking two more critical patients right now."

"Thank God."

"Asa and I split up to find you and Jackie, but he found you first."

Whitney's blue gaze stares up at me. "We have to go get your brother. We can't leave him here."

Pain and grief tears through me. "You're going in the ambulance with your aunt. I'll get my brother. I'll find you—"

"No," Whitney says, wrapping a hand around my arm. "I'm not leaving without you. Not now. Not ever."

Asa returns and drops to a knee next to his sister. "We gotta go now. You heard what they said. One road out; that's it. We need to move fast. Let's get your brother's body and get the fuck out of here."

WHITNEY

Two weeks later

THERE'S BEEN TOO much death. Too much loss. The wildfire consumed Commodore and Magnus's cabins, then jumped the river to destroy half the town of Gable before rain poured down in a deluge and helped put it out. Asa, Lincoln, and I were lucky to make it out alive with Harrison's body. The road was completely blocked by the time we tried to leave, but Lincoln's chopper pilot managed to come back for one last pickup.

If not for that, we all would have died that day. Instead, we escaped with nothing more than bruises that are already healing.

Now we stand on the charred grass of the cemetery, in front of headstones scorched by the flames, while we lay Sylvia, Jackie, and Harrison to their final rest.

One funeral. Two families. Something no one would have ever believed could happen.

Magnus and Commodore sit side by side, and we all

watch as our family members are interred. Sylvia's ashes and Harrison's casket in the Riscoff mausoleum, even though he wasn't a Riscoff by blood, and Jackie in the plot beside my parents—who she left in the river that night.

Everything my aunt said to me in the hospital has haunted me for the last two weeks. I still can't make sense of it. Can't process it.

How could she have done all of it?

Jackie passed away a week and a half ago after slipping into a coma on the ambulance ride to Rock Hollow. They said it was a bleed in her brain. She never woke up again. Now we'll never know the rest of what happened, because she can't answer any more of our questions.

Karma sits beside Cricket with her girls, who we now know are definitely Hunter's. Karma was actually the one who insisted on the paternity test, and the results came back positive a few days ago. Hunter sits on Cricket's other side, holding her hand. He's been a rock for her and the girls as they navigate this new reality.

Karma's surgery was largely a success, despite its hasty completion. She's going through chemo now, but the doctors seem confident she'll recover. The Riscoff Memorial Hospital didn't survive the fire, but Lincoln has arranged for her to be treated in Rock Hollow by a team of specialists.

Her attitude has changed so much in the last two weeks that I barely recognize her anymore. There's humility and sorrow, where before there was bitterness and anger. Telling her and Cricket everything Jackie had told me was one of the hardest things I've ever had to do.

Tears dripped down Karma's cheeks then, just like they do now as we say our good-byes.

Karma knew exactly what I was talking about when I relayed what had happened that night after Roosevelt hit on her at the bar. She told Cricket and me everything, including how, in her twenty-year-old idiocy, she'd been so proud and wanted to tell her mom. She cried even harder when she told us that Jackie had been livid, and she'd accused her mom of being jealous. Jackie had told her to find someone her own age before storming out, and Karma was too blinded by her anger to put things together about that night—that what happened in the bar had unleashed a chain reaction that ended with the deaths of my parents and Roosevelt. Instead, when Ricky came home, Karma clung to him when I didn't, and that's when her obsession started.

She apologized to me. She apologized to Cricket. She apologized to Hunter. Every single apology was completely sincere, even though all three of us stared at her like she might have been abducted by aliens and someone else was returned to earth in her body.

Lincoln stands when the preacher goes quiet, and I realize I've completely checked out of the ceremony. He leads me forward, and we both lay flowers in front of the mausoleum and the grave.

"This ends the Riscoff-Gable feud permanently. We've all lost too much. There's no more room for hate when it's time to build anew." Lincoln's voice rings out, and everyone in the small crowd gathered at the cemetery nods in agreement.

Cricket rests her hand over her belly, and I send up a prayer of thanks. At least there is one new miracle we can celebrate in about seven months.

From death comes new life.

LINCOLN

Three months later

By SOME MIRACLE, my home, my family's estate, and The Gables survived the fire. We've spent the last three months working on rebuilding everything on the side of town that wasn't quite so fortunate.

Riscoff Holdings donated every board we had to the construction efforts. The thousands of acres of timber we lost, while small in the grand scheme of things, made it even more imperative to me that we diversify. The deal that I'm closing right now will be one of my most important contributions to the next generation.

I scrawl my name across the bottom of the last document and look up at the two men who are now my partners in a new business opportunity.

"I look forward to what comes next, gentlemen."

Creighton Karas, the friend who was gracious enough to let us use his glass beach, stands up from his chair at the head of the conference room table. "I think we have a very profitable venture in our future."

Jericho Forge, the man who came through when Riscoff Holdings' bid wasn't submitted on time due to Harrison's delay, rises from his seat across the table. "I wouldn't have signed on if we weren't going to make a hell of a lot of money."

They're both self-made billionaires, men who have earned my respect, especially after negotiating with them to form this partnership. Karas's expertise comes from the financial side, and Forge is a shipping magnate.

Jericho Forge owns the world's largest commercial fleet, which is astounding considering he's close to my age and supposedly lived on the streets at one point as a kid. Rumor has it that he joined the merchant marines and somehow worked his way up to captaining freighters traveling highly dangerous routes around Africa before he started his own fleet. To look at him, I can believe every single bit of it. He's built like a longshoreman, but now instead of wearing a captain's uniform, he wears thirty-thousand-dollar suits and looks almost civilized.

Almost. Something about Jericho Forge will always remind me of standing in the presence of an untamed beast, which is great when he's on your side of the negotiating table.

"If you'd like to stay for tomorrow, we'd be more than happy to have you join us."

Forge shakes his head, and his long black hair brushes his collar. "Weddings aren't my thing, but I appreciate the offer. Best wishes to you and the future Mrs. Riscoff."

Karas grins. "Holly is thrilled that it's happening here. I've made her promise that she won't corner Whitney to talk about buying her songs until your next visit, however."

"I'm sure Whitney would be happy to talk to her anytime she wants. She's been writing a lot, and I know she wants to hear another voice on the radio singing her words."

"I think it's safe to say that she definitely will," Karas says.

The sound of a chopper interrupts our conversation, and we all look out the picture window of the conference room overlooking the ocean.

"That's mine," Forge says. "It's a pleasure doing business with you both. Time for me to get out of here."

Beyond the approaching chopper, at least a mile out from the glass beach below us, a mega yacht is moored, waiting for him. I suppose the rumors of him being more pirate than CEO could be true.

Forge rounds the table and extends a hand to me. "Congratulations, Riscoff. Enjoy the wedding."

I shake it, and he moves on to Karas.

"Still smug as hell about staying single, aren't you, Forge? Watch out, that just might be your downfall," Karas tells him.

The shipping tycoon booms out a laugh, his broad shoulders shaking. "No woman will be my downfall."

"Famous last words," I say, and he gives me a chin jerk before he leaves the room.

Karas turns to me as soon as Forge is gone. "How long before he eats those words? I'm willing to put money on it."

I consider the enigma of a man who strides toward the chopper beyond the window. "Inside of a year."

"I say six months, and we'll be watching him walk down the aisle," Karas says with a smug grin of his own.

"I'll take that bet." We shake on it. "Now, my beautiful bride should be arriving any minute with her family, and I don't want to miss the surprise on her face when she realizes where we're getting married. I appreciate the hell out of you letting us use the beach again."

Karas smiles. "It's our pleasure. Holly would've never let me say anything but yes."

"We appreciate it, and I'm sure Whitney will be thrilled to meet her."

WHITNEY

I SHOULD HAVE KNOWN that it would be perfect. Absolutely and completely perfect. Lincoln wouldn't allow anything else for our wedding.

Correction, our *double* wedding.

The rainbow of glass shimmers like multicolored gems beneath our feet as Cricket and I each hold Asa by the arm and walk toward the men we love.

My simple white dress blows in the breeze, and I'm overwhelmed with pure joy as I stare at Lincoln's smiling face waiting a few yards away.

When we stop before the grooms, Asa kisses Cricket on the forehead first, and Hunter takes her hand. If not for Lincoln's wide grin, I would have said Hunter looked to be the most excited groom on the planet.

Then Asa turns to me and squeezes both my hands. "I know when to admit that I was wrong, and I hope you'll forgive me. I just want you to be happy, Whit. That's all I've ever wanted."

"There's nothing to be forgiven. Not anymore. I love you, Asa."

My brother kisses my forehead and then looks to Lincoln. "This is how it was always supposed to be. Take care of her."

"Until my dying breath," Lincoln replies.

Asa gives us both a nod and steps back to join the small group of guests standing on the beach watching our wedding. McKinley Riscoff shifts nervously next to him.

Interesting . . .

Instead of the huge affair that Mrs. Havalin had pushed for, Cricket and I agreed that we wanted something very intimate and private, and no one was going to bulldoze us.

Asa, Commodore, McKinley, Magnus, Karma and the girls, as well as Hunter's parents and our hosts—Creighton and Holly Karas—stand witness to the ceremony, and it's absolutely perfect.

We say our vows as the sun goes down, and Lincoln freezes when the preacher asks if anyone has any objections.

Everyone laughs.

"No objections to this union. Not from a single one of us," Commodore says, his voice booming over the crashing of the waves. "This is the beginning of a new era for both our families. The best is yet to come."

And it is a beautiful new beginning. When Lincoln's lips brush mine to seal our vows with a kiss, I feel lighter and more at peace than I ever have in my entire life.

This is everything.

When he pulls back, he looks down at me. "Just wait until you see what we're having to eat for the reception. Then you'll really be impressed."

"What?"

"Torchy's Tacos. We flew them in, just for you."

My cheeks already ache from smiling, but my lips curve up even harder.

"Best. Wedding. Ever. And not just because of the tacos."

LINCOLN

Two years later

THE LAWN of the Riscoff estate is packed with people—friends, family, business acquaintances, and everyone in between. We started a new tradition last Fourth of July, and I think it's safe to say that it'll continue for many years to come. Kids run by with sparklers, and I look for my wife.

I find her on a blanket on the lawn where our little boy, Carter, crawls around while his cousin, River, toddles. Cricket and Whitney laugh as River tries to help Carter stand.

This is how it's supposed to be.

The next generation of Gables and Riscoffs are being raised together as family and will never know what it's like to be enemies.

Commodore and Magnus sit in their chairs behind them, watching the kids and tipping back their own drinks.

Whitney stands as I approach and rushes forward to throw her arms around me. "I just sold more songs!"

I press a kiss to her lips. "I'm so proud of you, Blue. Who this time?"

"Holly picked up two more, but she also brought Boone Thrasher and Ripley Fischer with her. They went through everything I've written in the last six months and were freaking out. Boone said he and Ripley are going to record 'Happily Ever After' next week so they can release it for their anniversary. How cool is that?"

"Amazing, which is exactly what you are."

"They invited us to the Grand Ole Opry to hear it performed live for the first time. How do you feel about making a trip to Nashville?"

"I'd go anywhere with you, Blue. You know that."

And we have certainly done our best to hit as many spots as we can, even while she was pregnant. Our honeymoon to the Seychelles was only the first place on Whitney's bucket list we crossed off. She doesn't know it yet, but I'm planning a trip to Easter Island next. But that can wait until after she conquers Nashville.

Rose, Creighton and Holly's daughter, runs past the blanket with Maddy and Addy not far behind. Karma, Cricket, and Hunter have worked hard to make sure they never want for anything, and Whitney and I have been part of that cause. After all, they're my nieces too. Laughter fills the air, and a feeling of absolute peace settles over me as I sit down and pull Whitney into my lap.

This is how it's supposed to be.

Someone produces a guitar, and moments later, Boone Thrasher and Ripley Fischer sing Whitney's song "Happily

Ever After" in perfect harmony while we wait for the fireworks to start.

I hold my wife tighter as part of the chorus washes over us.

I didn't know it when I stepped off that Greyhound bus,
But you showed me that we could live our
happily-ever-after . . .

THE END

ACKNOWLEDGMENTS

Another story on paper. Another journey complete. I swear, every time I start a new book, I wonder if I actually know what I'm doing. Even with almost thirty books under my belt, I worry every single time.

Thankfully, I have the most incredible team helping to make sure I keep delivering my best with every book.

Massive thanks go out to—

Pam Berehulke for helping me craft and fine-tune this story to be the best it can be.

Julie Deaton for making sure we caught every little thing in proofreading.

Jamie Lynn for holding down the fort like a boss while I disappear into the writing cave for days on end, and for all the million things you do.

Letitia Hassar for designing such gorgeous covers.

Danielle Sanchez for helping me find the best ways to share this story with the world.

All the bloggers who take the time to read and review simply for the love of reading.

All the bookstagrammers who take such gorgeous pictures of books and share your talent with the world.

My readers, who are the best in the entire world. I have so many things planned for you. Thank you for sticking with me on the ride. I promise the best is still yet to come.

And last, but certainly not least, my rock, JDW. When I lose my way, you help me find it. When I stumble, you lift me up so I can soar. Ours is my most favorite love story of all time.

ALSO BY MEGHAN MARCH

SIN TRILOGY:

Richer Than Sin

Guilty As Sin

Reveling In Sin

MOUNT TRILOGY:

Ruthless King

Defiant Queen

Sinful Empire

SAVAGE TRILOGY:

Savage Prince

Iron Princess

Rogue Royalty

BENEATH SERIES:

Beneath This Mask

Beneath This Ink

Beneath These Chains

Beneath These Scars

Beneath These Lies

Beneath These Shadows

ABOUT THE AUTHOR

Meghan March has been known to wear camo face paint and tromp around in the woods wearing mud-covered boots, all while sporting a perfect manicure. She's also impulsive, easily entertained, and absolutely unapologetic about the fact that she loves to read and write smut.

Her past lives include slinging auto parts, selling lingerie, making custom jewelry, and practicing corporate law. Writing books about dirty-talking alpha males and the strong, sassy women who bring them to their knees is by far the most fabulous job she's ever had.

She'd love to hear from you. Connect with her at:

Website:
www.meghanmarch.com
Facebook:
www.facebook.com/MeghanMarchAuthor
Twitter:
www.twitter.com/meghan_march
Instagram:
www.instagram.com/meghanmarch